About the author

John L Murphy is a clinical social worker by trade and a lifelong seeker of Divine Love at heart. His twenty-four-year history working in community mental health has been a commitment to offering support for suffering populations. John is motivated and driven by making every effort to follow Mastery in Servitude as shown by Avatar Meher Baba. Artistic expression, music and writing are vehicles for communicating the heart. John feels privileged to share his writing with you. It is his aim to intrigue, inspire and uplift each reader.

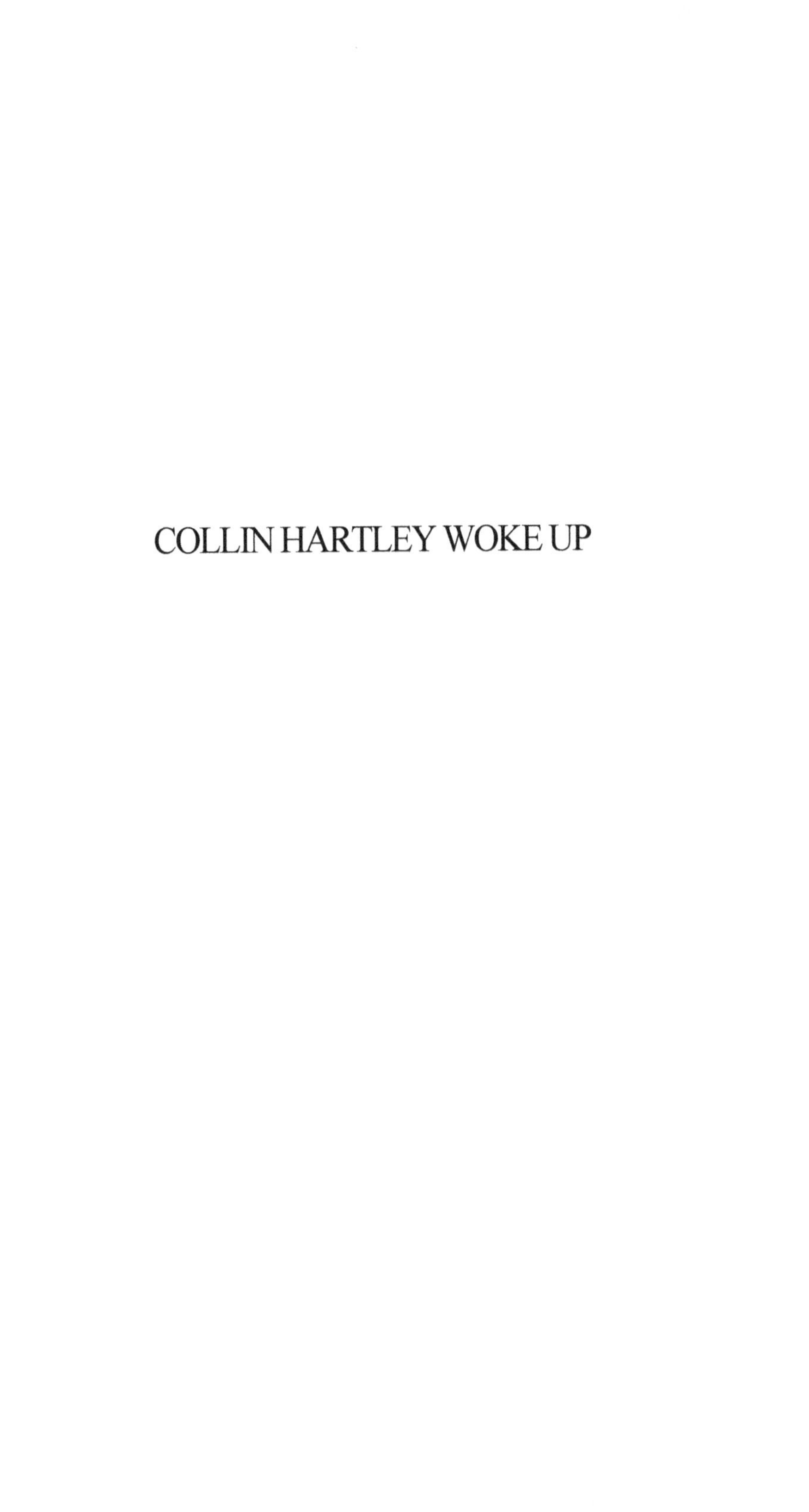

COLLIN HARTLEY WOKE UP

JOHN L MURPHY

COLLIN HARTLEY WOKE UP

Vanguard Press

A CIP catalogue record for this title is
available from the British Library.

ISBN 978 1 80016 313 3

*Vanguard Press is an imprint of
Pegasus Elliot MacKenzie Publishers Ltd.*
www.pegasuspublishers.com

First Published in 2022

**Vanguard Press
Sheraton House Castle Park
Cambridge England**

Printed & Bound in Great Britain

Dedication

The Compassionate Father. The Great Awakener.
Avatar Meher Baba.

Chapter One: The Bicycle

Collin Hartley woke up. He cleared his eyes and then focused his vision on the ceiling fan above. His sight, blurry at first, soon cleared and became sharp as a knife. The ceiling fan, like his own body, was moving at the slowest setting possible. It hummed gently as it turned around and around. The morning air was crisp, the mood was light and the room was rather cozy. Collin realized that he was lying awkwardly on his right arm. It was still sleeping even though Collin himself was awake, so he pulled it out from underneath with the opposite hand. His heart pumped fresh blood into the sleeping limb so the arm warmed up and then icy pricks ran up and down it like frozen rain. He took in a deep breath while those sensations penetrated into his bloodstream. Then he exhaled. He let go of not only the air but of his dreams as well. The dreams disappeared quickly into the ether of the bedroom. When Collin settled for a moment, he noticed an itch on his left thigh but he decided not to scratch it. He used that itch as a way to further awaken from his sleep. He could feel the dryness, the flaking and the chafe. The sensation seemed so small and insignificant at first, but then it took over the whole leg. The itch grew up and down the leg at the same time and then it spread throughout the rest of his body. That once small irritation then turned into a raging fire and rather than putting it out, Collin Hartley let it set him ablaze. He even grinned as the morning air fed the fire of that itch while it moved stealthily across his skin. Needless to say, at this point Collin Hartley was certainly awake.

After a few minutes of burning, he pulled himself out of bed and then went to the bathroom to clean up. Collin brushed his teeth, he urinated and then he stood in front of the bathroom mirror. He looked deeply into his blue-grey eyes and questioned whether he was seeing himself clearly. He wondered if he was out of focus or blurry. He wondered what part of himself he might not be seeing. He was sure that he was missing something, but he wasn't sure what that was. He was alive in the questions and the mystery. He kept on looking in the mirror but all he could see was the same old things. He saw the short brown hair, the ratty beard, the bad complexion and the stained teeth. Then he crossed his eyes some so that his vision would become totally blurred. He took in long, exaggerated breaths and kept staring but there was nothing new. Just a hazy face in the bathroom mirror.

When he realized how much time had passed, he reached in the shower and started running the water. He stepped in and covered himself with inspiration. The water was ice cold and just the way he liked it. Collin Hartley was an unusual character. He scrubbed his body in the same way that he washed the dishes: it was impersonal and it was as if his body was not his own. He lathered, soaked and then rinsed off the body in the invigorating sprays of water. Then he became so moved that he started singing part of a song from one of his favorite bands. Collin was stirred, stimulated and enthused.

He belted out over and over again, "Roll the windows down. This cool night air is curious. Let the whole world look in. Who cares who sees anything? I'm your passenger."

Collin stopped the shower, he dried off his body and then went into the east room of his apartment to complete his morning meditation exercise. He sat on a dented steel folding chair. It was the kind that would come with a cheap poker table. It was brown with some dried paint splashes. He relaxed his shoulders, straightened his posture and held his hands together gently in his lap. Collin began the exercise by concentrating on his breathing. Deep gusts of air moved in and out of his lungs. He closed his eyes and sensed his overall being. He moved his attention throughout the whole body doing the best he could to sense the self rather than drifting off into thoughts. Starting with his toes and feet he moved up through the body. His awareness was running its invisible hand up his legs, through the torso, the arms, shoulders and straight to the top of the head. Collin was experiencing the sensation of his entire physical body. He started with the outer and then moved towards the inner. Sensing his posture, his flesh, his muscle and his skeleton. And then deeper, sensing the blood as it coursed through his veins. Still deeper, Collin believed that maybe he sensed something finer than his own blood; it seemed more like a vibration. It was very subtle and most curious. He repeated his mantra over and over again.

"Infinite Power. Infinite Knowledge. Infinite Bliss. Infinite Love." And then, "I am The Infinite Within."

When the meditation was complete, Collin Hartley opened his eyes and he could see himself positioned in the great pattern of life. The blinds from the window were opened and the daylight came shining in. It seemed that the sun was touching everything. His hardwood floors, his cat, his computer and his physical self all bathed in light. And then he looked beyond, past his city block, past his own state and past his own nation. At that moment he sensed his connection with the entire creation. Collin Hartley was something and he was nothing at the very same time.

After completing the morning exercise, he left the east room and then walked into the kitchen still completely naked. He poured some water into his teapot and heated it on the stove. He sprinkled fresh green tea leaves into his favorite cup and started eating a bagel. The taste was incredible. It was honey wheat and his favorite texture of all. Collin chewed, savored and swallowed, the whole time wondering if the flavor filled his essence as much as the wheat filled his stomach. His taste buds were exploding. Then the teakettle whistled and he poured the hot water into his cup. No sugar was needed. It was quite simply the sweetest elixir imaginable.

After breakfast, Collin got dressed and prepared himself for a life amongst people. He reminded himself that all life was One and that he should work to see this as a reality and not as an obscure idea. He remembered that it was important not to think of himself as separate — a life of me and them — but to remind himself constantly that he is an integral part of a great cosmic pattern that he does not yet understand. He imagined himself as a lens that was being adjusted to perceive The Spirit That Moves in All Things.

When Collin left for work, he locked his apartment door and then headed down the stairs where he was stopped by a neighbor. She was leaving the building also and he sensed a connection with her through this simple commonality.

"Good morning, Mr Collin," she said with a peculiar smile.

"Morning, Ms Weeks," said Collin.

"I wanted to thank you, Mr Collin," she said, "for helping me with my car yesterday. I don't know what I would have done without you. I couldn't get it started and then you hooked up the jumper cables and vroom, vroom. I was on the road again. Oh, you were so nice to help me. So I made it to my job. And I may have been out big bucks if you didn't lend me a hand, Mr Collin."

Then she whispered, "So tonight I'll bring you some of my homemade pizza. As a special thank you. Just the way you like it. Soy cheese, artichoke hearts, banana peppers and garlic… absolutely delicious."

"Only if you join me, Ms Weeks," Collin replied. "Your company will be just as welcomed as that incredible pizza you make."

Ms Weeks howled with enthusiasm while she started rubbing both of Collin's arms. She shook her head as if bewildered by his presence and then she turned more thoughtful.

"Why don't you have yourself a nice lady, Mr Collin?" she said. "You're so handsome, so polite and so well mannered. You would make a nice girl so very happy."

"Who can say?" he replied. "Maybe it's for the better though. I think Tarazina might get jealous if you know what I mean."

Ms Weeks howled again and the vibrations from her laugh moved deep into the man Collin. He tilted his head downwards and opened himself up to that cacophony. Then he became like a tuning fork while he resonated the perfect pitch of her sound.

"Your kitty cat, Mr Collin," she inquired, "how is she doing?"

Collin moved towards the entrance of the building saying, "Still vain… still tons of attitude, Ms Weeks. Also, still full of love."

Ms Weeks patted Collin on the back and gave him a look of sympathy while they walked outside the building. It was as if she felt sorry for him that he was single. She reassured Collin that he was a good man and made it clear that she cared for him. But Collin walked on with a tender indifference. He just nodded his head while she spoke, he said goodbye to her and then headed in the direction of the brown line train.

While walking, Collin's attention ebbed and flowed between his own self and the world outside of him. He kept his eyes closed at first, sensing the movements of his body and observing the inner darkness. Then he opened them and saw children walking with their parents to school. He saw dozens of tall oak trees shading everyone using the sidewalk. He saw seated houses of great wisdom and he felt the eternal sky looking down on his neighborhood from above. Then he closed his eyes. He returned to sensing the movements of his body and his own inner darkness. Then he opened them and then closed them again. Each step was precious and each instance had something to be observed. Snapshot after snapshot, Collin walked on attentively.

He reached the station and took the train to the Belmont Avenue stop, then he headed to Renee's Restaurant where he would have coffee each morning with the Mysterious William Green. The two of them would sit together daily and talk over any number of questions regarding life. Collin entered through the front door and immediately noticed Willie's bicycle resting against their usual booth. Collin sat down and began observing the alterations Willie had made to his bike. The bicycle seat had been replaced with a flat wooden block that had a fine grit sandpaper stapled to the top of it. The pedals had been replaced with old glass Pepsi bottles and a saltshaker took the place of the usual water container. Collin chuckled to himself while he stared at this contraption. And after a few minutes Willie appeared and sat down across from him.

"What do you think of the changes I've made to my bike?" asked Willie.

"I'm not sure what to think," said Collin. "I think I like it… definitely curious and excited."

"Well, you're feeling anyway," said Willie, "at least you have that."

Collin leaned back and took in the presence of William Green. Willie's dark skin appeared tattered and dry, and it seemed to Collin that he had been well into the Golden Years. His beard was mostly gray and dreaded, yet his eyes were youthful and containing tenderness. Willie was careful in his movements, and he appeared acutely aware of his surroundings. He wore a long winter coat and a Chicago Bulls skullcap. Strangely he was also wearing thin exercise shorts and a pair of sneakers with no socks. This dress ensemble was bizarre since it was the middle of January and there was a foot of snow on the ground. Any other person might walk by Willie and label him obscure or homeless mentally ill.

"So, why the alterations to the bike, Willie?" Collin asked.

Willie did not respond at first; instead, he looked softly into Collin's eyes while the server poured them two cups of coffee. It was only when she left that Willie spoke.

"The seat is for discipline, the glass pedals for sensitivity and the saltshaker for denial."

Collin sipped his coffee and then replied, "I remember you once telling me that life is too comfortable. That it promotes sleep. You say that we are robots and that we roam the planet in programmed dreams. I also remember you telling me that I should strive to wake up… to awaken from these dreams. And looking at that bike, I'm wondering if it's some sort of waking mechanism. An awakening machine. I can't help but think that that's the reason you've altered it… as uncomfortable as it seems. To assist you in waking up."

Willie looked into his own cup of coffee and then closed his eyes for a moment. It was as if Willie had absorbed the vibrations of Collin's voice with every fiber of his being. Then he opened his eyes, he sipped his coffee and began speaking.

"I see that I lack many things. I lack understanding, I lack discipline, I lack sensitivity and I take for granted the things and the people who nurture me in life. So I'm taking the most uncomfortable seat in the house. I'm taking a seat that forces me to sit carefully and with right posture. I must be attentive in my positioning. I must pedal on with sensitivity and I must tread softly. I have to give way to every bump, ditch and obstacle that is on the way. Yet at the same time I have to continue in my direction regardless of the terrain. And my task is to pedal with the gentleness of a dove. I cannot remain the sledgehammer any longer."

Willie sipped his coffee and continued, "I must endure this great journey with patience and remain thankful for all of the guiding forces that show me the way, even when I am shown all of the dark and treacherous places. I will drink my water when I've reached the fountain. Until then I am thankful for the food that nourishes me on the way, grateful for the air in my lungs and grateful for the hope that drives this journey."

It was at that moment that Collin was struck with the idea that maybe Willie was truly someone with a psychotic disorder. Then he thought that he himself must also be psychotic for associating with him. He thought that only madmen could reason in the way the two of them did. And for a second Willie seemed crude, unrefined and even primitive. Collin looked at the bicycle, the way Willie was dressed and his overall demeanor, all of which, at that precise moment, struck him as being completely schizophrenic.

Then Collin's emotions surfaced and he could experience that they were feelings of love, commonality and hope. He saw two men fascinated with the human condition. Collin could feel Willie's struggle and his aim to awaken to something totally real. He loved Willie's work ethic, his creativity and he felt honored to be on the same team. Collin could see a subtle likeness during those moments. He saw two men talking and working on ideas that would seem ludicrous to most. These were two men who wanted to open up to the unseen but struggled with their dreams. And that conversation over coffee was somehow sacred like many of the other conversations they'd had over coffee before.

"Isn't life a struggle in itself, Willie?" Collin asked. "Without the added struggle of riding that bike all day long?"

"How comfortable are you?" Willie asked sharply.

"It depends," responded Collin. "Some days I feel all warm and cozy and other days I feel like the sheets have been ripped right off of me."

Willie dawned a grin that was distinctly his own. It was a sort of half-smile that exposed only two or three teeth.

Willie said, "And it's in those warm, cozy days where the sleep lies. Our sleep promotes dreams, dreams imagination and imagination lies. And there is nothing in half-sleep or half-awake. You have to strive towards one or the other. You must decide to be either totally asleep or totally awake."

Collin sipped his coffee and responded playfully, "So should we never sleep, Willie? Is that the key? To struggle continuously so that all that is left is a walking zombie?"

"We're already walking zombies," Willie replied. "And you shouldn't take my words so literally. Sleep is surrender and sleep is important. This is of course the sleep we take at night, and I know that you already know this. I'm talking about awakening from our waking sleep. Our waking sleep is the sleep walking, the sleep driving and the sleep talking that we do day in and day out. We're like mindless robots that bump into one another while carrying out these tasks. Hypnotized and monetized through the exchange of goods while playing to the lowest common denominator in life. Eat, drink, shit, fuck, sleep…"

Willie adjusted his Chicago Bulls cap and then continued, "You want to wake up, Collin, or you wouldn't be sitting here with me right now. You desire to get past the stale fogginess that is your perception of life. You want to experience what is Real and you want to become conscious of The Truth. You want an end to machine life and you want an end to monotony. But most important, you also feel drawn to the idea of a merger with the pure illumination of love. Soul Love! Life was not created for the Soul to remain stagnant and satisfied with dreaming and machining alone. It is designed for the realization of The Highest."

Collin chuckled to himself out of surprise. He had never heard the Mysterious William Green talk about love and this took him off guard. He thought about making a joke of it for a second but then he held his tongue. Collin remained silent and his quiet was the simple result of Willie's heartfelt expression.

"Have you ever lost anything, Collin Hartley?" asked Willie. "Has anything ever been taken away from you?"

This question took Collin by surprise. It seemed like a silly question to be asked. Obviously, he had lost things. He and Willie had been friends for a few years now. They knew many details of each other's lives. Intimate details. For instance, Willie knew that Collin's parents were deceased and that he was estranged from his family. He knew that Collin had lost friends, girlfriends, jobs, money and property. In fact, loss was a big part of Collin Hartley's life. He had little money, virtually no connection or close friends and he had few belongings. You could even say that his losses were the reason he embarked on the path of enlightenment. This was the reason he befriended Willie and had talks about subjects like awakening, Soul experience and Divine Truth.

Collin said, "You know all of my losses, Willie. You know that is a big part of my life. I have lost just about everything."

"Well not quite everything," Willie sharply retorted. "You know, The Avatar of the Age said that God helps the seeker by taking away everything in his path to The Eternal Ocean of Love. He clears the path when the aspirant is ready. When someone has the desire to wake up from the worldly life of gross objects then those things begin to disappear. The meaning of that dream fades away and the Real experience of Infinite Divine Bliss starts to take over."

"So all of my losses are part of my awakening?" asked Collin.

Willie replied, "Maybe it is better to see it as The Infinite removing the barriers to your Highest Self. In that way loss is not really loss. If you look at it that way then it is really gain. You gaining your Real Self. Then you see that The Compassionate Father is leading you to the most beautiful Soul experience. When you really want that experience."

Then Willie smiled slyly and said, "Maybe The Compassionate Father will remove more barriers on your path. To awaken from this dream," said Willie, "we must have the courage to sense our own suffering. To accept the importance of suffering. To see suffering as a symptom of transcendence. And accept that we are dreaming. The journey of waking up is a long and difficult road. It is an epic adventure that can happen in our everyday mundane existence. We have to sense with every cell of our being this folly of life. Only then can we be interested in something else. Everything we have experienced up until this point has been all dreams and imagination. And remember that this sleep is appealing because, as you said, it makes us feel all cozy and warm. I think it is hard to fathom what this sleep prevents us from becoming. However, with a wish, a desire to know what our possibilities are, and with the help of a good bicycle of course… we might just pass into the unimaginable. The Infinite."

The two of them laughed as Willie patted the wood seat of his bicycle. They could both feel the significance of their friendship and the high value of their brotherhood. Collin noticed that a couple sitting next to them looked on with confusion and it made him feel a little out of place. Willie and Collin just smiled at each other and then finished their conversation.

"Well, I'm off to work," said Collin while taking the last sip of his coffee. Then he stood up and tossed a few bucks onto the table.

Willie looked up at him and said, "I wish you well today, my friend. You are my friend and brother. I hope your adventures today are enlightening and fruitful."

"Thank you, Brother William," Collin replied, "and you be careful on that bike. I don't want to see you getting scraped off of Belmont while I'm coming home from work tonight. That thing is fascinating but also crazy dangerous."

Willie nodded, almost bowing as Collin made his way out through the restaurant doors.

Collin jumped back onto the brown line train and continued his trip downtown. He took a seat towards the back of the train; he closed his eyes and absorbed the vibrations of the voices that surrounded him. People were talking about sports, concerts, nightclubs and art. But he didn't place much attention to the content of what was being said. Instead, it was the tone, rate of speech and fullness of sound that he attended to. For just a moment he went beyond the subject and he could feel the love, excitement and energy being exchanged. At one point the sounds became orchestrated in the most profound way. This ensemble had an undefined feeling and it was difficult to categorize. The instruments were crude but the resonance, the actual quality of sound was most brilliant. It was rock-n-roll on an emotional level. The sound vibrations moved through his body in a subtle ecstasy.

It was the smell of pungent body odor that opened Collin's eyes. A homeless man dropped down on a seat next to him and the smell was overwhelming. It was like being buried in a mountain of soiled baby diapers while at the same time being sprayed with sweat. The shock made him gag but he somehow kept his composure. He looked attentively at the homeless man who was now bumped up against him. He was a white man with long, dreaded hair and a sparsely grown moustache. He was wearing several layers of clothes with an outer covering of army camouflage. His green coat was buttoned to the top and his army field pants were crusted all over. He had a toothless smile, bad breath and what seemed like hardened chili surrounding his lips.

"The angels told me you'd open your eyes today," he said to Collin plainly.

Collin just grinned as his thoughts branched out in front of his inner observer. Is this man for real? Why has he sat down next to me? Should I ask him his name? Should I ask about the angels? Should I get up and walk away? Or should I give this man a few dollars?

These thoughts appeared together, instantaneously in layers. He was aware of all of them, but he opted to choose none. He remained silent instead. It was an intuitive understanding that the homeless man should speak again.

"So," the homeless man said, "are your eyes open completely or are they only half-open?"

Collin, who was doing the best he could to control his gag reflex, replied, "Well, the important one is still closed."

"Yes," the homeless man exclaimed while kicking up some more stench, "these eyes that see brick, concrete, wheels, cars and streets don't mean a thing. Important to open the inner eye. The mind's eye."

Collin nodded his head in silent agreement while taking in the presence of his new friend. Yes, this man was odious, yes, he was awkward and unclean, but Collin felt a familiarity with him. In fact, he felt more himself in those few moments than he had amongst some of his own friends and family. It was a 'getting to the point' that seemed lacking in many of his other relationships. And after this realization, the foul smell even seemed to vanish.

Collin asked him casually, "So are your eyes half-open or are they open completely? What about your mind's eye?"

The man responded, "The important one is half-open. Just cracked a little bit like the important ears. They catch glimpses of the angels and hear words that these lips could never say."

Then he moved closer to Collin and said, "And in comparison to their language, we are like barking dogs, grunting pigs and ribbiting frogs."

Then he began looking around at other passengers saying over and over again, "Ribbit! Ribbit! Ribbit!"

Collin couldn't help chuckling as he saw the expressions from the faces of those around him. He saw eyes roll, heads shake and some drawn to criticism, all except an elderly woman who ribbited right back at the homeless man.

"It's like a wilderness out here, isn't it?" said Collin.

Then the homeless man started grunting like a pig and said laughingly, "I like to eat shit! I'm hungry for more! I'm hungry for more!"

Collin burst out laughing and grunted back at the man while those who were nearest to them got up and stood by the train doors.

At that point Collin became silent and sensed the playfulness he was experiencing. Surely, they were both psychotic. They were not oriented to the same experience as everyone else on the train. His inner critic called him a madman, but he didn't consider that voice much of anything. Instead, he felt love for the man next to him and love for those standing by the train doors. He felt love for the old lady who stayed near and love for the whole scene as it unfolded. Collin was outside judgement and preference.

Collin heard the conductor call out that the train was arriving at the Chicago Avenue stop so he stood up and bid the homeless man farewell. They shook hands and the man wished Collin a good day.

Collin jostled carefully down the steep stairwell until he reached street level. Then he looked ahead and was amazed by the organic web of life that moved about before him. He saw people talking, pigeons looming and cars racing before his eyes. Then there were the exhaust fumes, sewer mist and the noise pollution that seemed to gel the whole picture together. And he could see himself in the pattern as well. There was Collin Hartley, smiling like an imbecile on the great canvas of the universal dream. The contrast of Dark and Light was astonishing.

He was headed two blocks west towards the office when he overheard an interesting conversation between two men. The older of the two had gray hair, a plump build and stood no taller than five feet six inches. He walked silently with his hands held together behind his back and mostly listening to what the younger man was saying. The younger of the two was clean-shaven, he was thin with brown hair, and he seemed to tower above his friend.

Collin heard the younger man say, "I think that your average person misses the point of most fantasy novels. They are not books about literally slaying dragons, saving princesses and winning great battles. And they are not about literally finding treasures, magic rings or mystical scrolls. Those books are about defeating the dragons inside of us. They're about shining light into the dark cave that is our inner world. They're about eradicating the evil goblins that we have inside with the hope of discovering the mystical treasures buried further within."

The older man looked up at his friend saying tenderly, "Yes, fantasy novels can contain wonderful parables."

They both nodded in agreement while Collin followed behind.

"And the truth is," the younger man continued, "that the inner dragon is real. So are the goblins. This dark cave with its dampness and all of its internal pitfalls are very real. I could even hear those goblins this morning just after I got out of bed. Stay sleeping! Your job is stupid! Don't go to work! Everyone is out to get you! They want to gnaw at your flesh and chew on your bones! They want to rip you to smithereens!"

"And what of shining some light into this cave?" asked the older man.

"Yes," his friend responded, "it was the conscious recognition of this negativity that sent those demons scurrying. I could see those negative inner feelings and thoughts and that meant something. This light of awareness sent them away. But I know all too well that they'll be back. I seemed to have won a small battle today, but the war is still going on. The inner war is not finished until it is finished."

Then suddenly the older man stopped, he looked directly at his friend saying, "And someday our hero will find his hidden treasure… my fearless warrior… my son."

Collin passed by the two men while feeling grateful for what he overheard. He knew all too well the struggles with the inner dragon, the inner goblins and the inner darkness. This was the only war that existed and all the other wars throughout history were but projections of the very same inner war that continues even today.

Collin Hartley was not raised in the big city and it took him time to learn the Chicago habitat. He grew up in suburban Ohio. He played little league baseball, jumped ramps with his friends on his Huffy bicycle and strummed the guitar whenever he had a chance. Collin's dream was to be a rock star when he was a teenager. He loved to feel the angst, the freedom and the energy as it coursed through his fingers. He also enjoyed bonfires at the beach on weekends, camping and hanging out with his girlfriend. He had a fairly normal childhood. It was in his twenties that the suburban life started to change. He lost both of his parents to cancer within two years of each other. This put a strain on his family. He began seeing things differently from those losses. Collin started looking within and asking the big questions about life. Who am I? What is the aim of life? What is our highest potential? This changed his relationships with others and in some cases created total cut off. So Collin moved to the city. He wanted to go in a totally different direction than his life course in suburban Ohio. It was either the big city or total isolation in the Southwestern desert. Collin Hartley chose Chicago. His first few years were rocky as the pace was faster, the population denser and air more constricted. He had to learn public transportation, the neighborhoods, the people and how to get by on little money. In a way city life drove him further inside himself. The outer intensity pushed him within. However, he found his way in Chicago. He got an apartment, he got a cat and he bounced around from job to job.

He finally arrived at his office where he stood for a few moments and observed the sign above the entryway. 'Restful Eternities' was written in purple against a black backdrop. An engraving of the full moon hung above it and the sign was boxed in with a bronze border. Collin loved to look at that sign. It was a reminder of why he picked that job only one year earlier.

Restful Eternities is a small telemarketing company that sells grave plots by phone. They have a website and social media presence, but they still do some old school calling. Collin stumbled across the ad online and it asked for assertive callers eager to make as much as one thousand dollars each week. He always wanted to try one of those telemarketing jobs but he never followed through. He didn't even know they still existed. He wanted to interject some creativity while he interrupted your dinner at night and have you saying no thanks and please take me off of your calling list. So he finally gave it a try. And it was just the icing on the cake that this place was selling funerals.

Collin knew from the moment he started the job that it would be a perfect opportunity for spiritual awakening. It was a constant reminder that death can come at any minute and that we need to prepare for it in our own way. So it created immediacy in him; it was a driving force that seemed to propel his wakefulness. This job reminded him that every moment is an opportunity to awaken to something new and that he had no time to waste. Collin had seen enough of the transitory in life and he yearned for something more. He had seen things born and sustained only to die, and he knew that this was his fate also. Just as it had been for his mother, his father, his uncle and his grandmother. So Collin was attempting to look inside of everything. He worked to focus on the spirit. He desired to discover the Life that has no death, no birth and the Life that is beyond time. He swore that he could feel it moving through him and he longed to disappear into it like the moth vanishing into the flame. This was just the type of death Collin Hartley wished for. He wanted the sacred death that a person can experience while still in the flesh. It is the death in life that brings on the experience of Eternal Life. It is the Great Enlightenment.

After his pondering and reflecting about the significance of his job, Collin passed through the front doors and headed up the stairs to the second floor. He passed several rows of cubicles and heard dozens of callers pleading their sales pitch. He tossed his coat in the corner of his cube and then sat in front of the phone for a few moments.

He aligned himself vertically with perfect posture and then created a true symmetry of the body. His hands were folded in his lap and his gaze went upward towards the center of his forehead. He relaxed with his breathing and then closed his eyes. It was then that he felt higher vibrations moving inside of him. And after a few more minutes he felt as if he were a nebulous, where the beginning and the ending of his self was uncertain. Instead, he was like a cloud of energy that expanded in all directions. And the more he went inside, the finer the energy. Then he began to hear faintly inside of himself the words "I am". Then "I am" again.

"Do you hear me, Collin?" his supervisor exclaimed.

Collin opened his eyes, feeling unsettled by hearing his own name.

"I am going to give you one more week to make a sale," said Tim, "or I'll have to let you go. You've been here for one full year, Collin, and with very little to show for it. Sometimes I wonder how you can afford to pay your bills. You haven't made a dime here in months and I won't allow you to go on like this."

Then Tim relaxed a little and continued, "You're a smart guy, Collin, you should go back to teaching again. Or better yet, go to India and find a guru. Do something that's a better fit. I just don't think that this is the right place for you. You are way too eccentric and way too out of touch for something like this."

Collin cracked a smile as he thought about his last year as an art teacher. He really loved teaching, but his major complaint was that his students could not concentrate or commit themselves to finishing anything creative. He was mostly working with teenage boys from broken homes and tenuous family lives. He found himself resolving more conflicts with his students and talking with them about the various trauma of their lives rather than actually creating art. He struggled to help them channel their experiences into art. Collin found nothing but blocks and barriers. And he started to receive criticism from his principal about spending so much class time dealing with the behavioral issues.

Collin sometimes struggled with classroom management. This made him feel like a failure as a teacher.

Collin often chuckled to himself about the great education machine. He felt that the bottom line of production was the thing that the administration valued the most. It didn't matter that the kids were doing drugs, fighting or having sex between classes. Being a top academic school was most important and the principal wanted the student body to show academic excellence. Art was an afterthought. All Collin could see was the scared looks in the eyes of those teenage boys so he would spend class time trying to address some of their issues. Many of the students were in crisis, they seemed lost and they couldn't concentrate in class, so he tried to accommodate them.

At one point, Collin tried integrating the problems these teens were having through art lessons, but the principal became furious. He felt that Collin was trying to undermine the curriculum and destroy the integrity of the school. His approach was too bold, too forward and not productive. The truth is that Collin was only trying to make his art class a therapeutic and positive experience. But when some of the student artwork began depicting sexual and sometimes violent images, all hell broke loose. These works of art reflected the very culture that these students lived and it was too much for the principal to bear.

When people began voicing their concerns, the principal finally asked Collin to resign from his position. All of this seemed illogical to Collin who saw that the student artwork was only showing the truth of their culture. The artwork expressed the fear, the gluttony and the trite air of competition that comprises a day in American life. His students saw these things on television and in the world of sports, they heard these messages through music and through arguments between their parents and they felt all of this stirring inside their selves like a restless storm. Collin only helped to bring these things to light so they could be seen and worked with. But his efforts were in vain and the result was his being dismissed from his role as art teacher. So he left the school and decided to try working in an environment that was completely new and not experienced by him.

Collin began each call with a variation from the standard sales pitch. It's one that Restful Eternities suggests to each worker. Collin's own unique deviation of this pitch starts:

Good afternoon, sir or ma'am. I am Collin Hartley from Restful Eternities and I'm wondering if you could answer a question for me today?

And if the person on the other line did not hang up, he would continue:

I'm wondering if you have considered the inevitability of your own death and how that will affect your loved ones when you are gone.

And if they were still on the phone he would continue:

We here at Restful Eternities would like to lift the burden of death from your family. We would like to add comfort to your day of dying by setting aside a humble space for your mortal remains. Yes, sir or ma'am, we have acre upon acre of green rolling hills that echo the melodic sounds of ever flowing fountains that will calm your earthly leftovers. When your soul moves on from this life, we would like to take care of your body by placing it in our own little piece of Heaven. And by placing five hundred dollars down today, you can let the worries of death fade away. With this payment you will be well on your way to making your funeral less stressful for your loved ones. We here at Restful Eternities can handle all of your funeral preparations far in advance. We will arrange a burial place, a headstone and even a casket for your dead body. And if you'd like to be cremated, we can assist in those preparations as well. Why have your family stress and obsess about these details when we can resolve all of this today? By working hand in hand with you, Mister or Misses so and so, we will make the day of your departure free from all anxiety and free from financial concern. Are you interested in these wonderful services that Restful Eternities can provide for you today?

So it's really no mystery why Collin was at the bottom of the sales board and why he was also disliked by his supervisor. But the most appealing part of taking the job in the first place was that Collin was given the freedom to say just about anything he wanted on the phone. All his supervisor cared about was sales. Tim's only concern was the bottom line, and it wasn't until Collin went several months without landing a sale that the threats of being fired started.

So as usual, Collin's first few dozen calls that morning were all busts. He was mostly hung up on, but a few did ask to be taken off of the calling list. However, Collin didn't sweat these things since he knew that it all came with the territory. So he kept up the calling with the same enthusiasm as the first day he started.

It was around ten o'clock when he got his first bite. He was naturally excited, since it was the first one he'd had in a month. The call started out shaky, but Collin persevered.

"Hello," he heard from the other end.

"Good morning, sir," said Collin. "I am Collin Hartley from Restful Eternities and I'm wondering if you could answer a question for me today?"

"Sure," the man responded as he slurped some sort of beverage, "why not?"

Collin continued, "I'm wondering if you have considered the inevitability of your own death and how that will…"

Immediately John began laughing so Collin stopped. He even started to chuckle with John and then waited for a response.

John said, "Wow, this is the best hassle call I've ever had. What in the hell are you selling?"

Collin set aside the scripted sales pitch and replied, "We here at Restful Eternities sell grave plots, headstones and caskets."

John's laughing turned into a cackle and he replied, "Okay, I'll play along. But I'm only twenty-five, man, and though I've thought about dying, I haven't thought about where I'd be buried. Or what my headstone might be… or a casket for that matter."

Collin became more thoughtful and asked, "So what comes to you when you think about dying?"

John's laughing transformed into a chuckle and he said, "Well, I guess I think about the people I've known to die first. My family… friends… acquaintances. I wonder about them. If they're alive somewhere else… what they do there… what their experience is."

Then John's chuckle turned into relaxed sincerity and he continued, "So then I start thinking about life. It's funny how thinking about death always makes you think of life. You can't help but search for purpose. Why do we walk this earth? Why do we live and die? What is the meaning of all this?"

"I wonder those same questions," said Collin.

Then John took a sip of his beverage. It was not the slurp that Collin heard only a few moments earlier.

John asked, "So have you come up with any answers?"

"Mostly questions," replied Collin. "Mostly questions and observations. I am a seeker."

"My grandmother used to tell me," said John, "that life was about learning how to be the perfect lover, to learn unconditional love. It seems such an impossibility but I'll be damned if she didn't make the impossible seem possible at times. Biggest heart and most loving person I have ever known."

John paused and then asked, "What do you think, Collin? Your name is Collin, right?"

At that moment, Collin thought about his own grandmother and the love that she had shown to her family. He remembered her gentle ways, her reassuring looks when loved ones were in crisis and the way she could see hope in the ugliest of situations.

"Yeah," said Collin, "why is it so hard for us to love openly like that? Is it because we are men? Is it because we are afraid of other people? What jades us? What callouses our hearts?"

"I take things too personally," said John.

"Me too," Collin replied.

Then John continued, "I have this notion that everything is about me. When life is good then it's good for me. The sun is out, the birds are chirping and everything is just roses. All for me… and when life is bad, well then that's all for me too. The sky is clouded, the birds are muted and everything is just shit. All for me…

"See," John said, "I forget about other people and I lose sight that I occupy space with other human beings. I mostly live for myself. If things are good, then I don't need anybody. But when things are bad, well that's a whole different story."

Collin asked, "Who do you love most in the world, John?"

John took another sip of his beverage while he thought it over.

"My brother," he said, "my dad and my buddy George."

"And are these the people you console with when things are bad?" asked Collin.

"Among many others," replied John humorously.

"How often do you go out of your way to make life good for your loved ones?" Collin inquired.

"That's a tough one," John said. "My dad and brother live out of state and my buddy George… well, George doesn't really need anything."

Then John stopped abruptly and replied, "But I get what you're saying. And you're right, I should make an effort. But like I was telling you, I rarely think about how I can make life better for other people. Remember, it's all about me."

Then John changed the topic of conversation by asking Collin if he believed in God.

Collin smiled to himself and then answered, "I have to believe in God."

"What do you mean?" John asked.

"Well," said Collin, "I'm beginning not to believe in this life of limitation, so what other choice do I have but to believe in God? God is The Supreme Existence. God is Infinite. Beyond limitation. Everything is contained within God. Otherwise, God would be limited. Those are the words of Meher Baba. The Great Awakener. We attribute infinitude, timelessness and omnipotence to God.

"The life of God is a life of freedom, bliss, power and understanding. And as I see myself believing less and less in this life… the life of birth, death, high, low, good and bad all boxed inside time and space, it's only natural that I would begin believing in something else. I want to be free, I want an end to pain, I don't want to fear anymore and I want understanding. I long more and more each day to merge into those Godly attributes, and I have to believe that this is possible. I don't see it as a choice."

"So, what do you think?" asked John. "Do you think that this life is a sort of road that takes you there?"

"Something like that," said Collin. "But in my opinion, it's more that this life is the symptom of our soul becoming something beyond the body, beyond energy and beyond the mind. God, Infinite Love, Infinite Consciousness are all beyond the body and mind."

"Is that Heaven? Do you think that we can reach Heaven before we die?" John inquired.

"I think Heaven and Hell are karmic experiences," responded Collin. "We travel through Heaven and Hell to reach the highest. I think The Infinite guides us to reach Absolute Bliss before the death of the physical body."

"Man," John said, "how can anyone actually do this in reality though? I think it's impossible. Maybe in thoughts and dreams it's possible... more like a theory... and even then, probably the theory and dreams of a madman. Only fooling himself..."

"I've been told those same things many times over," Collin said, "but that doesn't mean it's true. Everyone lives the ordinary life. However, there is also the possibility of living the Extraordinary Life. We are living the ordinary life anyway. We all eat, sleep, socialize, have hobbies and work. We can also have this other journey as well. The spiritual journey. They are not mutually exclusive. The spiritual adventure can happen while we dream the Earth Adventure."

Then Collin softened his tone and continued, "I get glimpses of a spiritual life that I don't really understand with my mind and these glimpses show it's a higher life. It's freer, it's lovelier and understanding happens with the heart and soul in that life. And it's those glimpses that drive me to see more. Maybe trading in our old eyes for new ones."

"I see the same old crap day after day," said John. "Sure, I have good days where the crap seems more polished but really it's the same old thing. I work, I eat,

I converse, I eat again and then I sleep. What else is there?"

"Good question," said Collin, "and the way towards its discovery is to continue looking. To continue observing… to keep asking."

"Seek and ye shall find," replied John. "Isn't that what they say?"

"Exactly," Collin said, "but the difficulty is in the complete follow-through of our seeing. We're mostly half-assed. We have no real drive to see more than we can. Usually, we're content with the surface things. We're quite happy with the reflected images of birds on pond water."

"Do you think it's fear of going deeper or maybe fear of the unknown?" John asked while taking a careful sip of his beverage.

"It's my opinion that fear plays a role," replied Collin. "And we have to observe our fear like anything else. If we can see and understand our fear, then maybe we can get past it. And that's a part of every great adventure. The hero must first see and have a real understanding of the obstacles (in this case fear). Only then can it be overcome. With no shortage of inside and outside help of course…"

"I fear myself in many ways," John said. "I've got some crazy thoughts, paranoid delusions and depressed attitudes in me at times."

"Be grateful you see these things," said Collin.

"Grateful," expressed John. "How can I be grateful for seeing that ugliness?"

"Because without seeing your demons you would never be able to get past them," Collin explained. "They're all imaginary anyway. None of it's real. Even so, you have to see these self-constructed nightmares in order to wake up from them."

Collin softened his tone again and continued, "It takes courage to face these hallucinations. So, keep the faith and keep looking. Believe it or not there's hope in this seeing."

"And how in the hell did we end up talking about all of this?" John said quite suddenly. "If I remember right you were trying to sell me a funeral."

"I still am," said Collin jokingly, "and for only five hundred dollars down today, I can secure you a little piece of Heaven for your mortal remains."

John laughed hysterically

"Let me get this right," John asked, "I give you five hundred dollars now and you'll reserve a burial space for me?"

"That's right," said Collin.

"So what about the headstone, casket and the remainder of what I'll owe?" John asked.

"Well," Collin said, "if you would like to put your money down today, I'll transfer you to one of our customer service reps and you can talk over the details with them."

"Don't most people want to see the grounds first so they can see specifically where they'll be buried?" inquired John.

"Yes, most do," said Collin.

"I think that's what I'm going to do," replied John.

"Okay," said Collin, "well I'm going to pass you on to one of our customer service guys, and they'll finalize everything for you."

Then there was a silence between them while Collin thought over some appropriate words of departure.

"I hope you keep seeing, John, and I wish you love and prosperity in your journey."

Then John replied awkwardly, "And I hope that you experience the Extraordinary Life, Collin Hartley. I hope that you will see with your new eyes and that everything in this mundane life disappears for you, along with your old eyes."

"Peace be with you, friend," said Collin.

"And peace be with you," said John.

Collin pressed the button that would transfer the call to customer service. He hung up the phone and reclined in his seat. It was then that he could see Tim from out the corner of his left eye.

"I can't believe you roped a sale with that line of garbage," Tim said while shaking his head in disappointment. "What a line of crap. You know that sale is not final. You don't need to let it all hang it all out there for everyone to hear, Collin. Because I gotta say… what you have to show is kind of scary."

Collin just smiled and thought to himself silently, "I'm clothed before men, Tim. I'm only naked before God."

Chapter Two: The Bed

Collin Hartley woke up. He felt his body pulse rhythmically beneath the soft cotton sheets. The feel of the linen was comforting, and he felt caressed as if living inside a wooly cocoon. There was also a simultaneous discomfort and coldness as he soon realized that he was not in his bed. Collin's backside was pressed against the hardwood floor and his cat was licking at his toes. He pushed his palms down flat on the ground and rubbed them over the polished surface. Collin kept his eyes closed while he smiled and contemplated why he was lying on the floor.

At first, he thought that maybe he fell off of his bed overnight. It would not have been the first time that this happened. Collin remembered drunken nights and hungover mornings where he fell out of the bed sometime between the sun falling and the sun rising. Then he considered that maybe being on the floor was from sleepwalking. He had been known to sleepwalk in the past, also associated with drinking, and he had in fact woken up in many unusual places. As Collin thought over these scenarios, he continued feeling around the ground with his hands. He wanted to wait a moment before he opened his eyes, so he first oriented himself with this new position through his sense of touch. He wanted to exploit the sense of touch as much as possible. Collin moved his hand across the floor, then slowly up through the sheets, and across his chest. He registered the sensations as his hands crossed each new surface. Then it ended when Tarazina came close to his face and rubbed her soft fur across Collin's cheek. At that point he couldn't help but open his eyes and take in her presence. It was upon opening his eyes that Collin noticed his bed was missing altogether.

"Where did the bed go?" Collin asked Tarazina.

Her round yellow eyes peered back magnificently at Collin while she purred quietly. Her black coat hung like a mink and her feline gestures exaggerated her femininity.

Collin sat up and began looking around his bedroom which was missing its centerpiece. The apparatus for sleep, comfort and rejuvenation was gone. It was like a hole dug in the middle of a garden. It was a barren and empty plot surrounded by life. He had never observed the room from this point of view before and the perspective excited him. Collin felt that something incredible was beginning and he looked on with wonder and curiosity.

Then the questions branched out in front of his inner observer; they were multiple and they appeared instantaneously in layers. What happened to my bed? Where did it go? Was it purposely taken from me? Did it dematerialize by my own accord? Why did I not wake up when it was removed? What does this mean?

At that moment Collin knew that he had to share this information with the Mysterious William Green. Willie was his guide, his mentor and his go-to for questions of the unknown. Collin felt restless and anxious about getting to Renee's Restaurant as soon as possible. He still had his morning routines that needed attending and he wanted to stay disciplined to get those done. So he got up and went about his business. All the while, nervous energy surged through his body. At times it even seemed that his spirit wanted to jump right out of his flesh so that it could go and meet with Willie independently. But Collin collected himself, he set priorities and he began to work through a compromised version of his morning routine.

Collin skipped taking a shower that morning and went straight to making his breakfast. He prepared his tea and bagel like he did every morning, but his thoughts continued to revolve around the missing bed. He thought maybe he was still dreaming. Then he questioned if he was having a psychotic episode. His mind stirred while his teeth mulled over the bagel. Half-finished consuming his breakfast, Collin realized that he was losing out on savoring the flavor and texture of his food. He was even standing up and pacing while he chewed and swallowed. So with this observation, Collin took a seat at the kitchen table and ate his meal properly. He absorbed the aroma, the taste and the texture of the whole breakfast. He became present and totally in the moment. This settled him for a few breaths but then he remembered that he forgot to complete his morning meditation.

Collin felt immediate disappointment by being swept away with his restless feelings. He knew that it was best to do the morning meditation before he ate, and he could see his lack of self-discipline through this experience. At first, Collin thought maybe it would be best if he skipped the exercise. He thought that missing one day would not be a big deal. However, Collin redirected and decided to do the exercise anyway since he felt it better to follow through with this daily discipline rather than passing it by altogether.

From the time Collin sat down on the dented steel folding chair up until the exercise was completed, he felt the anxious energy continue to move through him. Static vibrations echoed through his blood and bones. His thoughts raced with questions and then mental pictures of a future talk with Willie played out like a movie in his mind's eye. But Collin still took the posture, and he began by sensing his overall being. He started moving his attention throughout the whole of his physical being. All of this was very difficult since Collin's emotions and thoughts continued to be volatile. This created a burning in the man Collin since he focused on keeping the body still and symmetrical. He knew that a wiggle of the toes or a shaking of the legs would comfort him, but he refrained from any body movements. He refused to submit to any erroneous wiggle. He stayed disciplined, and by the end of the exercise his emotions became stilled and his thoughts less chaotic. Nothing is free. The kinetic energy of his restless thoughts and feelings fried the oily residue and devoured itself. He was more settled now.

"Infinite Power. Infinite Knowledge. Infinite Bliss. Infinite Love."

I am the Infinite within.

Collin arrived at Renee's Restaurant at about the same time he did every day. Everything was the same; the cozy booths were against the walls, round tables strewn throughout the center and the Mysterious William Green in the far back corner. As Collin walked towards Willie, he could see that the bicycle was still intact with all of its alterations. He sat down across from Willie, doing the best that he could to remain poised in this midst of his new experiencing.

"Good morning, young man," said Willie as he sipped on his coffee.

"It's a curious morning," replied Collin.

"Are you seeing things anew?" asked Willie.

"My bed disappeared overnight," responded Collin.

The Mysterious William Green nodded his head in what seemed like fatherly understanding. He smiled and then asked Collin to tell him more.

"I woke up on the floor in my bedroom," explained Collin. "I was lying in my sheets and the bed was gone.

It's exciting in a way. It seemed then, as it does now, that I have a mix of anxiousness and also curiosity. I can't help but wonder what this means."

"Have you ever been camping?" asked Willie.

With that question, a flood of memories came gushing into the presence of Collin Hartley like cool winds on autumn nights. They were recollections of camping trips he had taken with his dad and his brother many years earlier. The feelings of caring and tenderness came over him as the faces of these two men appeared in his mind's eye. He saw the three of them as a group pitching tents, building fires, laughing together and swimming in remote rivers. Then he heard the voice of his now deceased father telling him how proud he was of his two boys. Collin saw the men in his family closing their eyes at night to sleep amongst the pine trees, the wild grasses and the starry worlds.

"I used to camp a lot when I was younger," replied Collin. "The last time I went into the woods was about six or seven years ago. It was just before my dad died."

Willie drew in a long and steady breath, then he exhaled in a warm and quiet spirit. He looked compassionately at Collin and then began speaking.

"There's something wonderful that happens when you sleep directly on the earth at night. Your body is pressed close to her body and the only thing separating you two is this thin layer of flesh. There are no floors, no frames, no box springs and no mattresses between you. It's just you and her pressed together naked in the night."

"I miss it sometimes," said Collin, "being out in the woods. It's really as if nature is talking to you. It's a quiet yet profound voice. It's the voice of the trees, hills, plants and flowers. And the wind moves through you like a spirit. It's like the breeze cleaning your insides. The air is fresh, the water invigorating and the sky endless in its wisdom."

"Sleeping on a bed at night is like wearing a condom during sex," replied Willie as if he didn't hear a word Collin had said.

"What's that?" asked Collin who was unsure whether he heard Willie correctly. He chuckled.

"Really," said Willie, "it takes away all of the sensation. It numbs the whole experience. A bed deadens the resting experience just like a rubber numbs the sex experience."

"Are you saying that I should sleep outdoors?" asked Collin.

Willie took a sip of his coffee as a server came to the table and poured a fresh cup for Collin. When Collin leaned forward to smell the aroma of the brew, Willie responded.

"I've been sleeping at Margate Park in Uptown for ten years. Or maybe. It's that I've been slowly waking up in Margate Park for ten years. There's something to be said for living out in the natural elements. It takes a tremendous effort just to survive from day to day. And if you have the right attitude, this can be a very good environment for waking up. A life that's too comfortable just makes you want to sleep."

Then Willie paused for a moment while he thought over his next series of words.

He continued, "Though we all have to live our own lives. It may not be best for you to go sleep in the park. Your bed has dissolved and many more comforts will dissolve for you. So you should continue living in the elements natural to your own life. Be as it may. Let your life happen."

"In a way I feel like it's Christmas, Willie," said Collin, "only instead of receiving gifts, I have had something taken away. I feel like jumping up and down. And rather than begging, give me more, give me more… I'm saying take more, take more…"

Willie chuckled at this and replied, "Ask and you shall receive. But don't think it's going to be easy. This is only the beginning. You have asked the Compassionate Father to help you awaken. To help you transform… and you will, but only in good time and only through the fire of transformation. Enjoy this excitement while it lasts. The Christmas hangover is just around the corner."

Collin sipped his coffee as those last words played inside him like a tune, and it was then that Willie's bicycle caught his attention. Collin had not yet considered seriously what it must be like to ride that contraption. He could see by observing it that Willie would have to captain it just right. He would have to sit on it in just the right way and he would have to be acutely aware of his surroundings while the bike was being directed. Willie could really get hurt if the bike was not driven cautiously. If, for instance, Willie hit a large bump in the road, his rear and his feet could really suffer. It seemed to Collin that any major impact would shatter the glass soda pop pedals and then Willie's feet would become subject to injury. And the sandpaper on the newly constructed seating apparatus could turn his rear end into Swiss cheese if he had an accident. Needless to say, Collin was convinced that this new bicycle could only be directed with real attention and with an incredible perception of one's surroundings.

"Tell me the secret to riding that bike," asked Collin.

Willie turned to look at the bike and then he glanced back at Collin saying, "That bike can only be driven perfectly. Anything less than perfection, and you'll sustain an injury."

Then Willie held his cup of coffee just below his mouth and continued, "The trick, however, is to ride the bike on terrain that is in accordance with your own skill level. For instance, my own skill level at this time involves riding only on sparsely traveled side roads and some parking lots. I walk the bike everywhere else. I can ride it perfectly when there is little traffic and when there are few hazards. That is my current skill level. When I become completely acclimated to this skill level, then I will move on to the next. At that point I will begin with short stretches on Belmont Avenue perhaps. You see, any mistake made on this bike has the potential for disaster, so I need foresight in where I will be riding it."

Willie sipped his coffee and elaborated further. "The pedals of this bike have to be turned just right and I can sit on this seat only one way; all the time, the saltshaker stays on my mind. Too much force from my legs and feet, and the glass will break. Too much leaning to the right or left and my butt will ache. The whole of each ride, I am parched with no water to drink, but that's why I constructed this thing. I'm riding it towards the living waters and I will drink from them in good time."

Collin paused for a few moments as Willie's words absorbed into his blood. Collin could actually feel Willie inside himself even though his physical body remained seated opposite to him.

"How long does it take to awaken?" Collin asked.

Willie, who seemed to be looking over Collin's head, replied, "Everything is waking up. That's all that is happening. Waking up. Slowly over time. Rocks waken to tress, waken to worms, waken to bees, waken to monkeys, waken to human beings. Most begin with glimpses. Just little seconds where consciousness is heightened… and as you keep waking up, those glimpses will increase and turn into minutes. Then the minutes collect and turn into hours and so on. And the way that I understand it to be… when you fully awaken, time does not exist at all. Glimpses, minutes, hours and days vanish. Time disappears. But this is not important right now. Just words and experiences of the Awakened."

Collin took his last swig of coffee and then signaled for the server. He paid her for the coffees and then stood up.

"I think this is the beginning of my waking up," Collin said to Willie.

"All you have been doing is waking up," responded the Mysterious William Green.

Collin said a final farewell to Willie and then headed out the front door of Renee's. He stood on the sidewalk at the entrance of the restaurant for a few minutes; he closed his eyes and sensed his erect posture. He could feel random tensions throughout his back. He kept his eyes closed, slowly exhaled and felt the tension leave his body as the air slowly left his lungs. Afterwards, Collin opened his eyes to survey the urban landscape. Everything seemed the same as it ever was, only something was different about the mattress shop across the street.

As Collin crossed Belmont Avenue, he could see the absurd new reality of the mattress store. The storefront as well as the entire selling floor was completely void of all bedding materials. There were no beds, no frames, no box springs, no mattresses, no bunks and no futons. There were only people acting out bed sales and deliveries. In fact, one of the delivery workers almost ran Collin over with an empty dolly as he was leaving the store. So Collin backed away from the storefront while three delivery guys loaded phantom beds into an enormous truck. Then Collin looked back into the store where a young couple was finishing up a ghost sale. The young man paid the store manager for a beautiful king-sized nothing, and then the two of them pretended to carry it out the front door, the young lady holding the door for them both. It was all nothing into nothing.

"I'll pull my van around," Collin heard the young man say as he jogged off towards his vehicle.

The young lady looked at the store manager and said, "Thanks again for all of your help. We've needed a new bed for a long time now."

"My pleasure," the sales manager replied, "and remember to tell your friends and family about us. I can cut them a good deal too. You're gonna be sleeping good from now on."

Collin considered joining the role play but he wasn't sure if this was a good idea. He wanted to be as genuine as possible and he felt that joining in on the phantom mattress sale would only belittle everything. He knew that he was an indirect part of the scene by serving as a bystander and maybe that was good enough. He was hesitant about becoming more active. He was thinking that more direct involvement would only turn things into a joke. He felt this would make a mockery out of the people playing in this illusion. Collin thought he'd be toying with the play and that he would somehow ruin the picture.

Then he redirected and thought the opposite. Maybe it would be better to join in, yet at the same time work not to let on that he was privy to any special information. Just have some fun. This would mean participating in the phantom mattress business as if he also believed that these beds actually existed. Although Collin knew that this would be challenging. He imagined that it would be like interacting with imaginary friends while not letting his real friends catch on to the interaction. He would have to play a part that blended well with the overall scenario and at the same time try not to raise any suspicions.

So Collin strolled into the store and began looking around the empty space. Luckily there were still price tags in all of the places where real beds once rested. He moved around from price tag to price tag pretending to look over each bed.

"You're a king man," he heard from behind.

Collin turned to find the same man that helped out the young couple just a few minutes earlier.

"My name's Al," he said while extending his hand towards Collin, "and I can see by the expression on your face that anything smaller than a king has no interest for you."

Collin shook Al's hand while smiling and waiting for him to continue his sales pitch.

"Well," said Al, "you're looking at a real beauty, my friend."

Then he stepped towards the space Collin had been looking at and started bouncing his hands in the place where a bed once existed.

"Yes, sir," he continued, "this is about the most comfortable king made in the universe. It's good on the back and it's also good on the wallet."

Collin was struck by the movements of Al's hands against the invisible bed. It really seemed as though something was there. His hands appeared to depress and then spring up as if he were really bouncing them on a mattress.

"Go ahead and hop up on 'er," Al said. "I think you'll find this one very comfortable. Fit for a king!"

Collin thought what the hell and he threw caution to the wind. He jumped up and dove towards the bed, but he crashed awkwardly to the ground. He started laughing while he looked up at Al and waited for a response.

"Now isn't that the most comfortable damn bed you ever bounced on?" stated Al.

Collin picked himself up from the ground and replied, "Yeah, that's really something."

"If you'd like we can have 'er boxed up and shipped home by the end of the day," said Al.

Collin paused for a moment to consider his options. At first, he thought that it might be interesting to purchase this ghost and to explore the events connected with the sale. Then Collin realized that it would be pointless. He wasn't really interested in the outcome of the sale. Collin just wanted to interact with the phantom mattress event and that's all. Now he was done so he opted not to buy the ghost bed and he continued on with his day.

"I think the king is going to pass," Collin said while impersonating Elvis.

Before he left the store, Collin told Al that he was price shopping and that he'd be back only if he decided to purchase the bed. Al gave him a business card with his name and The Bed Zone embossed across the top of it. Collin took the card and then headed downtown to work.

The whole train ride consisted of thoughts and meditations on the significance of the vanishing beds. Collin's excitement and enthusiasm turned restless since he didn't understand what any of it meant. He seriously considered that he was going mad and that he would end up at the psych hospital before the week was through. He felt helpless and even a little frightened at times; after all, nothing like this had ever happened to him before. He lost his sense of control and he knew that he would be losing even more as future events unfolded. Was he ready for all of this? Could he handle more loss and more changes?

Collin exited the train and then stopped in for a cup of tea at a coffee house a few doors down from Restful Eternities. He took a seat by the front window and looked out while he savored the taste of his chai. He saw all the various expressions of mood in the faces of the passers-by. He saw couples smiling, friends laughing and a homeless woman praying. He saw the shrewd faces of businessmen, the raised eyebrows of lawyers and the beady eyes of art collectors. He also noticed that those dealing in money had almost visible numerical figures running across their foreheads. The art collectors had the words 'Beautiful' and 'Mine' in each beady eye and the lawyers with neck ties reading 'I am the law'. All the while Collin was struck by the love and laughter that resonated from the friends and couples that moved like ether in between the businessmen, lawyers and art collectors. He sipped his chai tea, feeling a true commonality with this scene. All of these aspects were within him also. The laughter, the tenderness, the greed and the pride were all things that he had experienced at one time or another. Collin Hartley filed these observations inside himself and then headed out the door for work. He was more settled, less anxious and ready for work.

He entered the calling floor of Restful Eternities where he was immediately detained by Tim.

"That's one hour's worth of calls you owe me, Collin," said Tim.

Collin felt irritated at first and he almost told Tim what he felt. Collin heard the words piss off, who cares, and you don't pay me enough, swooning through his innards. But those emotions prompted him to look more realistically at his situation. He was in fact late to work and there was no justification for this. He felt a little ashamed and irresponsible.

"I apologize, Tim," he said, "and I'll stay an hour later to make up for the lost time."

"That's good," replied Tim, "but with that crazy sales pitch you've got, I don't know if it's gonna make a difference anyway."

Collin just nodded his head in agreement and then walked to his cubicle. He moved in three dimensions of space, but it seemed only two dimensions of time. The future was before him and the past behind; it was his NOW that seemed to be missing. He did not experience himself as being grounded.

Collin sat down in the oversized caller's chair and his attention was then directed towards a paper he had hung on the wall. It was right next to the typed-out sales pitch, but the contents of this paper were very personal. On it were the eight points that Collin Hartley was to practice and remember each day. They were prompts to help him practice what's important. One could even say that this paper represented a part of his religion. The eight points were his credo.

1. Be Here Now
2. See The Spirit That Moves in all Things
3. Be happy and make others happy
4. Struggle with your habits
5. Do not display negative emotions
6. Repeat the name of God daily

7. Do not put GOD to the test

8. Practice 'Be As It May'

Collin couldn't help but smile to himself as he knew the absurd ambitiousness of being able to carry out these eight points. He had experienced time and time again the strain of even making efforts with one of these points. Sure, Collin liked to think that these tasks were easy but then again Collin was a master at lying to himself. Something as simple as not displaying negative emotions proved to be tremendous work. Collin remembered times in the past when his negativity was displaced all over creation and that when he began making efforts not to display this negativity, he thought he would explode. He recalled moments of holding in anger, frustrations and judgments. Then he learned how to pass them away inside, but then other negative feelings would appear in new guises and masks. So the simple work of not displaying these feelings became more complex and trickier than he once thought. And this was only one of eight points; all of them taken together seemed impossible. However, Collin Hartley was a determined man and he occasionally leaned on his sense of humor while the impossibility of carrying out these eight points overwhelmed him.

He thought, "What did you get yourself into, Collin Hartley?"

And he responded, "I don't know, but I'm finding a value in this. I don't think there's any turning back now."

Then he thought, "Look at your life. Your bed is gone… you consult every day with a homeless man about spiritual direction… you have no friends… you have no wife…"

And he responded, "Be happy and make others happy. Live this adventure and practice Be as it May."

"At what cost?" he replied to himself sharply.

"At the cost of everything," he heard himself say. "Everything I think I understand… everything I think I am… I tell you, Collin, I feel like the one weeping alone in the desert… and I ask, 'What kind of stone asks to be polished but complains when it is handled roughly?'"

And it was during these inner exchanges where Collin felt his true helplessness and his complete sense of contradiction. The tears welled up in his eyes and he could feel the inner crying throughout his self; and then the phone rang. He felt he was losing his mind and on the verge of a panic attack.

Collin stared at the phone as it vibrated, and he was hesitant to pick it up. He felt emotionally unstable and inept to handle any kind of business that would result from answering it. But then he concentrated three of his eight points, specifically to See The Spirit that moves in all Things, be happy and make others happy and Practice 'Be As It May'. So Collin found a hope in reiterating these points to himself and he picked up the receiver.

"This is Collin Hartley from Restful Eternities," he said in a quivering voice.

"Hello, Mr Hartley, my name is Danny Alvero from Somber Incorporated and I wanted to talk with you about an incredible investment opportunity this morning."

Collin couldn't believe it; in all of his time at Restful Eternities, he'd never received a telemarketing call. It seemed ironic and he felt for a moment that maybe he'd entered the Twilight Zone.

"What kind of investment opportunity?" Collin asked.

"The best kind," said Danny. "It's an investment in good sleep. Perfect sleep, in fact…"

"I'm not sure I understand," Collin replied.

"Well," said Danny, "we here at Somber Incorporated have developed a bed that will revolutionize the world of sleep. This new creation is something that no one has ever seen and it's going to change the way people rest at night."

At that point Collin was certain that he'd entered the Twilight Zone; it was that or he was truly losing his mind. An immediate rush of fear came over him as he felt himself going insane. Then that feeling vanished and it was replaced by an unexpected calm.

"Please tell me about this bed," requested Collin.

"This bed, Mr Hartley, is truly something from the future. It's a sleeping device that you might see on *Star Trek* or the like. It would seem science fiction and that's going to be one of its selling points."

"Is this futuristic bed affordable?" asked Collin.

"It's cheaper than your average waterbed," replied Danny, "and our bed won't make ya seasick."

Danny started laughing hysterically and Collin couldn't help but smile to himself. Do they even make waterbeds any more? At that point Collin decided to be creative with the experience. He chose not to judge it and to simply stay alive in this perception.

"So, tell me, Danny," said Collin, "what makes this bed so futuristic and so different that it would warrant an appearance on *Star Trek*?"

"Well, I'm gonna tell you, Mr Hartley," replied Danny, "but first you've gotta promise me that you're sitting down… because what I'm gonna tell you next will make you vertigo."

"I'm sitting," said Collin. "I'm strapped in and secure."

Then Danny expounded, "The Levibed Millennium is so new and original that one can barely find words to describe it. First, this bed has no box spring, no mattress and no frame. And when it's placed in your bedroom, it could be overlooked altogether. Imagine, Mr Hartley, a five-foot by seven-foot rectangle, no more than two inches thick, lying flat on your bedroom floor. Then envision this rectangle emitting electromagnetic currents that levitate the sleeper a few feet above it. Do I have your attention now, Mr Hartley?"

"Yes," responded Collin, "yes you do."

"Well, Mr Hartley," continued Danny, "the Levibed Millennium is a device that levitates the sleeper in mid-air and it can be adjusted for either a single person or for a couple. It's designed so that your sleep at night is perfect whether you are alone or with a loved one. Our scientists here at Somber Incorporated have fine-tuned the emissions of these electromagnetic currents so that your spine remains perfectly straight and the body itself perfectly symmetrical. Furthermore, the Levibed Millennium also regulates body heat."

"It regulates body heat," Colin interrupted. "How does it do that?"

Danny explained, "Well, besides the electromagnetic currents, the Levibed Millennium simultaneously radiates thermal vibrations. So, when these thermal vibrations resonate into the body at different intensities and intervals, they automatically influence body temperature. So, in the summer, you can adjust these thermal vibrations to cool the body down, and in the winter, you can adjust them to warm the body up. And I must say, having a Levibed Millennium myself, that you can regulate your body temperature to your own ideal. Really, it's the perfect night's sleep."

"You have a Levibed Millennium yourself?" inquired Collin.

"Yes," Danny replied, "the wife and I have been enjoying our Levibed Millennium for over a year now. It's one of the many perks of working for Somber Incorporated. You get access to products before they are introduced to the public."

Then Collin told Danny that his bed had disappeared overnight. He offered up this information out of sheer experimentation. Collin disclosed this fact only as an ingredient to the conversation and he was most curious about the results of this admixture.

"Well then, now would be a perfect time to invest in the Levibed Millennium," replied Danny.

Collin redirected and asked, "What would you do if you woke up in the morning and your Levibed Millennium was gone?"

"Ya know," said Danny, "that's the great thing about the Levibed Millennium. It's like you don't have a bed at all. It's the freest and most sublime sleeping experience imaginable. The wife and I talk about this often. We could never go back to the old box spring and mattress set-up."

Collin felt challenged by Danny's answers, so he decided to try a different approach. He wanted to open up the conversation and explore the importance of beds and sleeping. And Collin felt that this was a grand opportunity since Danny seemed competent and knowledgeable about the subject.

Collin asked, "Is it possible that we should not sleep so soundly at night? Could it be that beds promoting even deeper sleep, are actually harmful?"

Collin was then surprised by Danny's silence and he could almost see the void of Danny's blank mind.

Collin continued, "And I'm curious about this owing to observations I've made in my own sleeping habits. For example, I've found that when I'm out camping and spending my nights sleeping in the woods, that I tend to wake up earlier; I wake up invigorated, energized and ready to take on any work that needs to be done. However, sleeping in the woods is not as comfortable as sleeping in my bedroom. I average less hours of sleep when I'm outdoors and they're not as sound as the sleep I get at home. When I sleep at home, I'm truly comatose. I mean, when I sleep at home it's so deep and appealing that I find it hard to get up in the morning. I simply don't want to get out of bed. So, I wonder if it isn't actually better to sleep on harder surfaces and in a place that doesn't make your sleep seem like death."

Danny cleared his throat and said, "Maybe that's just it, Mr Hartley… maybe it's more about your sleeping environment and not so much about what you are actually sleeping on."

"What do you mean?" asked Collin.

"Well," continued Danny, "maybe you wake up more invigorated in the woods, not because of your bedding… maybe it's because of your surroundings. Being out in nature can be a beautiful experience. Maybe it's the fresh air… the feeling of being on vacation… the sense of freedom that comes with being away from your normal life. So then maybe you wake up at home unenthused and tired because you're sick of the monotony of your daily life. Maybe you don't want to get out of bed in the morning because you already know the repeating cycle that is your life. Again, all I'm suggesting is that maybe your quality of sleep has more to do with the environment and less to do with what you sleep on."

Collin smiled to himself while he gently nodded his head. Danny brought something to light that the man Collin had not considered. He even thought that maybe the disappearance of his bed was more of a prompt to look at his routines and the habits of his outer life than it was to ponder over the significance of a good night's sleep.

"So how can I test out your conclusions?" asked Collin.

Danny was hesitant to respond at first but then he replied, "It just so happens, Mr Hartley, that Somber Incorporated has begun manufacturing the Levibed Adventurer. It's smaller than the original, it's lightweight and it's collapsible. The Levibed Adventurer has been custom designed for outdoor expedition. So, I would suggest trying out the Levibed Adventurer both outdoors and indoors, then you could formulate a more objective assessment about your quality of sleep in both environments. In this way the Levibed Adventurer would act as a catalyst in your experiments. It would be a constant in both sleeping environments."

It was then that Collin noticed a distinct change in Danny's voice. Danny had clearly lost the enthusiasm he once possessed at the beginning of the call. His tone was now very sterile and matter of fact. This observation tugged at what Collin believed was his conscience since he felt this shift in mood was due to his own line of questioning. Collin knew the salesman persona all too well and he realized that he was pushing Danny a little outside his role through these questions. So Collin decided at that moment that he would reconcile his own feelings by purchasing the Levibed Adventurer and investing in Somber Incorporated.

"I believe you're right," said Collin. "I think I am going to invest in Somber Incorporated and the Levibed Adventurer."

"Very good," said Danny in a more chipper tone.

"So how does this whole thing work?" asked Collin. "I've never invested in a product before."

"We'll start you off with a trial of the Levibed Adventurer," Danny said, "and if you like it and believe it's a quality product, then we'll talk about your level of investment."

"Sounds good," said Collin.

Then he gave Danny his address and credit card information, the whole time wondering if the Levibed Adventurer would even make it to his doorstep. After all, it seemed that beds were vanishing everywhere and Collin didn't believe the Levibed Adventurer would be the exception. He knew that he'd have to wait it out and see if the bed would be delivered at all. However, it was Collin's opinion at that moment that it would not.

When Collin hung up the phone, he immediately noticed Tim standing by the entrance of his cubicle.

"So, now we're buying items by phone rather than selling them," Tim said coldly.

"That'll be two hours I owe you," replied Collin.

Tim shook his head asking, "Did I hear you right... did you just buy a bed that's supposed to levitate you in the air?"

Collin chuckled, "Yes... I just bought a Levibed Adventurer."

Tim put his hands into his pockets and replied, "You're a sucker. I don't think I've heard of anything more absurd in my life."

"You don't think selling grave plots by phone is absurd, Tim?" asked Collin.

Tim fidgeted and said, "We do a service to families here, Collin. We help to ease the burden of death."

Collin explained, "Well, Danny at Somber Incorporated is helping families to ease the burden of restless sleep. He's selling them a product that will give them a better night's rest."

Then Collin turned to his desk and looked over his call list for the day.

Tim walked away saying under his breath, "I gotta get this Danny character to come work for me. I could really use a caller that knows how to close a deal."

Chapter Three: The Chairs

Collin Hartley woke up. He felt groggy and he was apprehensive to start the day. He was experiencing some of the pangs of missing a good night's sleep. Collin could feel the immediate irritability and the sting of knowing that he had to face the world in this state. He sensed static energy moving about his insides and his eyes felt dry in the morning air. As he looked around the bedroom, he noticed Tarazina purring from the doorway. She seemed content and without a care in the world. So Collin tapped his hand on the hardwood floor and signaled her to come near. She obeyed his command and then scrambled to his side. Collin Hartley lay there on his bedroom floor covered in sheets while petting his beloved Tarazina.

"I'm feeling grumpy this morning," he said while running his fingers over the top of her head.

Tarazina buried her face into the sheets and continued purring while Collin petted her. She felt appreciated and comforted.

It was then that Collin remembered to be happy and make others happy and this freshened up his situation. He remembered that his life was changing and this created an excitement that was previously lacking. He could see himself, as if maybe it were the first time, petting his cat and beginning his day. This simple exchange of love stirred a new energy. The possibilities seemed endless, so open and so full of hope. He felt that anything could happen and that things could only be for the best. The air was fresh, the mood now cheerful and the atmosphere much lighter than when he first awoke.

"Well, little lady," he said to his cat, "I can't lay around all day in these stale sheets. I have a life to live so I'm gonna get busy livin' it."

Collin popped up from the ground and began folding the sheets. As he folded them, it seemed that his back was straighter than usual and his body more properly aligned. This made Collin happy and he thought that maybe sleeping on the ground wasn't so bad after all. Then he started whistling the song 'Waiting for the Miracle', by Leonard Cohen, as he fluffed his pillows. When Collin finished, he walked into the living room where his feelings changed abruptly once again.

All of Collin Hartley's sitting furniture was gone and a new wave of anxiety came over him. The couches, the corner chair and even his little wooden footstool were all gone. The only things that remained in the living room were the lamps, the coffee table, the drop carpet and the entertainment center. This unexpected scene sent restless energy currents through his body. He felt his hands turning cold and clamming up. He sensed his legs quivering and he noticed a spasm at the back of his neck. Then familiar thoughts came to him while he looked out at his half-empty living space. What does this mean? How should I respond? What is going to disappear next?

After these questions, Collin went about to investigate the rest of the apartment. He discovered, in fact, that all of the chairs in the apartment had vanished. The kitchen chairs, the lawn chairs on the back porch, the computer chair and even his dented steel folding chair were all gone. The only form that resembled a chair was the toilet, which he immediately sat upon and began his process of conflicting thoughts.

He thought first that he must be losing his mind, but that thought was countered by the notion that he was only lacking a clear understanding of the situation.

He thought second that he was cracking up and would be unable to carry on as usual around people, but then a tiny voice suggested that if he placed faith in his new perceptions, then all outside dealings would have absolutely no effect on him.

And he thought third that maybe he should reconsider going into work. He thought he should at all costs avoid going about his daily routine, but then another voice suggested that he should continue with his life as normal, beginning with a shower and his morning exercise.

All of these thoughts taken together propelled the man Collin into action, so he undressed and started his shower. And this shower seemed more personal than the one he had taken a few days earlier. His body still did not feel completely his own, but he did observe that he cared for it more than previously. He saw the quivering, the fear and the shame of the body, and he cleaned it as if giving it reassurance. In that moment there was an intimate love between the Soul of Collin Hartley and Collin Hartley the man.

After the shower, Collin went into the east room of the apartment to complete his morning exercise. Only this time he sat on the ground rather than on his folding chair. He sat cross-legged with a relaxed yet vertical posture, and with his hands resting on the knees. He began by placing attention on his breathing without altering it in any way. Then he sensed and relaxed the whole. Collin exhaled tensions and inhaled pure consciousness, then he closed his eyes and moved about the body while sensing each part. This was particularly difficult for Collin owing to his restless state. He wanted to move and fidget but he struggled to keep still and symmetrical. All of this created internal friction, but this fire only warmed him and shaped self-confidence. It was the self-confidence of the provision ego of the spiritual aspirant.

When Collin finished the morning exercise, he went into the kitchen to eat breakfast. He heated up the teakettle and prepared his honey wheat bagel, all the while naked as the day he was born. When everything was ready, Collin consumed his breakfast as he gazed outside the kitchen window. He noticed a few kids taking the alleyway to school while he chewed on his bread and sipped his tea. The kids were playful and this brought a smile to Collin's face. Love washing over Collin Harley. He couldn't help but remember the times when he was a kid, walking to school with his younger brother. He could see the two of them wrestling and he could see himself hit his brother jokingly in the rear with his book bag. Then this memory disappeared. Collin took the last bite from his bagel and the last swig from his tea while the kids from the alleyway disappeared from sight.

Collin dressed himself in the bedroom while staying concentrated on the sensing of his body. The sensing of the body stopped him from drifting off into the thoughts and ideas connected with the vanishing of his furniture. He felt subtle vibrations move throughout his flesh and it seemed at times that he was sipping on his own blood like wine. This new center of gravity turned the restless energy into a more focused beam of perception.

Collin left the apartment while he searched for new information concerning his condition. Like a detective, he was taking notes and making observations each step along the way. He was curious to find out whether anything else had vanished from his outer life and whether there were other people experiencing the same thing. He closely watched the people he passed by on the way to the train and he was confident that he'd be able to spot a person whose outer life was also dissolving. However, he didn't notice anything in particular; everything seemed the same as usual. Collin saw the same faces and the same occurrences that he did on all of his other morning walks to the train. Although, as he made the turn onto Irving Park Road, he did notice that the bus benches were missing. He could also see that all of the people on the passing busses were standing, which only brought him to the conclusion that the buses were without seats also.

Then Collin Hartley noticed something very interesting about the people he saw driving cars. All of the car seats had disappeared, so it took two people to operate each vehicle. He saw a Tesla pass by and could see one person kneeling and steering the car while another person worked the accelerator and brake. And this was the same for each car, truck and SUV that passed by him. Everyone in these cars carried on as if nothing was out of the ordinary.

When Collin arrived at the train platform, all of the benches were gone, so he stood with a group of people who were waiting to head southbound. A few minutes passed and the train pulled up where the group then boarded. Collin entered the train, where everyone was standing of course, and he took it to the Belmont Avenue stop where he met Willie each morning for coffee.

Collin Hartley passed through the front doors of Renee's Restaurant and immediately noticed that Willie's bike seat was intact. Then he turned to look at the bike rack outside the front windows of Renee's and he could see that all of those seats were missing. This naturally struck him as being odd. He wondered why all of the other bike seats had disappeared yet Willie's remained.

In this curious investigation of bicycle seats, Collin had overlooked one important detail; everyone at Renee's Restaurant was sitting on the floor while enjoying their breakfasts and group conversations. He saw servers kneeling to pour coffee and he saw bus boys scrambling on the ground to collect dishes. As Collin walked through the restaurant, he observed the Mysterious William Green sitting effortlessly in a perfect lotus position. Willie sipped on his coffee in the shadow of his bicycle while Collin approached him.

Collin sat down across from him cross-legged and asked, "How are you able to get that posture, Willie?"

"Good morning," Willie replied as he smiled at Collin. Then he asked, "Have you ever made a bow, Collin?"

"A bow," replied Collin, "you mean like a bow for shooting arrows?"

"Yes," said Willie, "a bow like that."

"No," Collin responded, "I've never made a bow. I have used one before though… I've just never made one."

Willie explained, "Making a bow with your own two hands is a real craft and it's one that takes the right preparation, the right commitment and the right amount of time. First, you have to seek out a piece of wood that will work well as a bow. You want to find a piece of wood that's neither too green nor too dry. Once you select the proper wood, you have to peel the bark off of it and then cure it in the sun for a day. After it cures then you can shape it as artistically yet practically as you like, so long as it serves its purpose. Then you set it out in the sun for a few more days so that it can season. After it seasons, you warm it by the fire and you grease it. Then a day later you repeat the process. Finally, after all this preparation and all of this work, you can string it up and call it a bow. Before this time, it was merely a work in progress."

Collin looked down at his own legs and he was sure that they would break if he tried the lotus position. Then he thought about Willie's allegory and felt it would take him years to even prepare for such positioning.

"Yes indeed," Willie said, "those brittle sticks would snap if you tried shaping them now. Remember that it takes the right preparation, the right commitment and the right amount of time. And that's if you even want the darn bow in the first place."

Collin chuckled as he looked up at the bicycle and remembered the question about the seat. While a server knelt down to pour Collin his coffee he asked Willie, "I can't help but wonder why your bike seat has not disappeared. You see, yesterday it was my bed that vanished and now today it's the seats that have disappeared. All the couches, chairs, benches and even bicycle seats… that is, all of the bicycle seats but yours, Willie."

Willie looked directly at Collin and it seemed that he was trying to communicate something to him through his BEING alone. Collin could see this intention clearly, but he still did not understand.

Collin said, "I've been asking myself the same questions now for many years. What does it mean to wake up? Who am I really? What is my sense and purpose in life? How can I work to be a better human being in its fullest sense?"

Collin sipped his coffee and looked out the side window of the restaurant continuing, "I have no answers, so I follow the example of the Souls who knew. I take to heart the words of Buddha, Jesus, and Meher Baba. I do my exercises, my tasks and I live by a certain code. All in an effort to tread the same path that those enlightened Ones showed…"

Willie smiled at Collin and he remained silent. It seemed that he was prompting Collin to continue with his discoveries.

"And wouldn't you know it," said Collin, "I'm getting cold feet just as the results of those efforts are beginning to show. I can see the fear and the helplessness of the unknown laid out before me. I am changing. Things are disappearing and I know that this will go on until there's nothing left. At times it scares me… but at other times I'm ecstatic."

Then the two of them turned quiet together for a few moments. They drank their coffee and savored the taste of each sip. Finally, Collin said some parting words before he left for work.

"I want to thank you for meeting with me this morning, Willie; I guess this is also a thank you for all those other mornings too. You've been like a teacher to me over the years. You're also a friend. You are my brother. You've helped me to stay directed and warm hearted in my spiritual aims. I just wish that I knew how to repay you."

Collin stood up after he placed the money for the two coffees in the middle of the sitting space. He zipped up his coat and put his hands in the front pockets.

The Mysterious William Green looked up at Collin Hartley and said, "Have a good workday… and don't worry about repaying me personally. Our friendship and company is proof of Infinite Divine Love. When the time is ripe, you'll settle your account by serving others. Mastery in Servitude, Collin Hartley. Remember Meher Baba. The Compassionate Father. An ambitious goal for any one of us to achieve. Master your service to others."

With that, the two nodded at each other and then Collin headed to the train. He trudged through the snow and then boarded a scarcely filled car. He stood towards the center where it seemed most warm. The mixture of the caffeine with his nerves made his insides feel like flames, so Collin turned his attention towards his breathing as a way to calm himself.

Then several questions appeared. He asked, "What will be next? Will it be the teakettle? Will it be Renee's? When will Tarazina disappear? What about Willie?"

"You have a lot on your mind," he heard from behind.

Collin turned to find a tall, professionally dressed man looking at him with sympathetic eyes. The man was wearing a black suit with a North Face coat over the top. He was meticulously groomed and it seemed to Collin that this man could have been a movie star. His brown hair was combed back, he was clean-shaven and he had a million-dollar smile.

"I'm Adam," he said.

Collin introduced himself while the two shook hands and it was at that point when he remembered to feed his heart. He began by asking himself how he felt about this scene and the response was marvelous. Collin felt a love for being conscious of even the simplest of things. The smell of Adam's cologne, the colors from posted advertisements and the motion of the train itself were all magnificent. He felt a love of being conscious of spatial relationships, the contrast and even the light that surrounded him. Collin's mind even started to quiet down as his love of being conscious was felt throughout the whole of himself. Then Adam asked him a question.

"Are you a writer, Collin? Maybe an artist... a philosopher..."

"I like to think I am," responded Collin. "The movie star in my head... you know."

The two laughed together and then Adam commented, "Yeah, I guess we'd all like to see ourselves as writers, artists and philosophers. Movie stars. The imagination is boundless. I like to think of myself as simply 'a man with knowledge'… and that's truly being creative…"

Collin replied, "It's interesting, this notion that we know anything at all really. Just when you think that something is known, then something else proves it wrong. I remember once believing that if I could just find the 'good' in everything then everything would be just that. Everything would be 'good'. And for the first month of this discovery, I believed that I had solved a great problem of life. I was seeing nothing but 'good'. Everything was 'good'. I felt that I really found gold… I could even see the 'good' in things like murder, war and car accidents. I just didn't question any of this. I was set on everything being 'good'. But I missed something important during this great discovery of mine. At some point, I wasn't able to carry the weight of such a simple solution. After all, some things are just 'bad'. And the 'bad' is important because it is there for comparison to 'good'. The 'bad' helps us appreciate and recognize 'good'. Something else was building up inside of me and I couldn't see it because all of my attention was on this 'good' business. I had to find the value of 'bad'."

Collin looked into Adam's eyes and continued, "I was put in my place at that point. I was reminded that this awakening process is a learning process. Constantly exchanging on realization with another realization."

"At least you have sincerity with yourself, Collin," responded Adam. "Obviously a restless mind… you are a seeker and adventurer."

Collin smiled at Adam and asked, "Are you a writer, Adam? Maybe an artist… a philosopher…?"

Adam nodded his head and said jokingly, "The movie star in my head… right."

Then Adam became more thoughtful and asked, "Why is the mind so quick to put forth any run-of-the-mill answer to our questions? It always wants a definite solution and at times it seems only interested in immediate pacification."

Collin cleared his throat and responded, "I believe it takes time to train the mind not to be so quick in constructing answers. To teach the mind how to really meditate on a question can be a life's work."

Then Collin looked curiously at Adam and asked, "Do you have any questions that you meditate on? Do you have any questions that are alive and not so easy to resolve?"

"Oh yes," said Adam. "The questions, who am I, what is my purpose in life and what is beyond the human experience are all constants. As well as, how can I work not to judge others? How do I remove the plank from my own eye so that I can help my brother remove the speck from his eye and how can I do to others what I would have them do to me? How to best live the

Golden Rule. These are all questions that are very much alive in me. At times anyway…"

At that point the train made a stop and Collin was in awe of all the movements that came with it. Some people left the train, others boarded and still others relocated throughout the car itself. It was an interesting series of actions almost like a ballet. The two remained quiet while Collin stayed attentive to this remarkable dance. It was simple yet it reminded him of a well-choreographed musical where each actor played their part perfectly. However, the music here was silent and the actors had no idea that they were on stage at all.

Collin broke his silence and said, "I also meditate on who am I, what is my purpose in the world and what is beyond the human experience. I also see answers coming to me… but they do not necessarily satisfy the questions. As you said, the questions stay very much alive. They escape the death that an answer brings."

"I'm curious," said Adam, "what kind of answers come to you? I know they don't always satisfy your questions… but I am wondering what these answers look like?"

Collin, who was still attending to the jostling movements that surrounded him, replied, "When I ask who am I, the response, you are Collin Hartley, of course, comes to mind. Then I answer further… you are this body, this heredity, these feelings and these thoughts. Then I ask, what of this consciousness that is in observance of these bodily sensations… this consciousness that observes these emotions and these questions of the mind. And the reply… you are that also. But my thoughts get stumped when I ask, what is consciousness? Is consciousness solely a brain function? Is consciousness more than brain function? Does consciousness exist after the death of the physical body?"

Then Collin looked at Adam and asked him sincerely, "Really, what is this consciousness? Who can accurately describe or define it?"

Adam, who was smiling, replied, "Of course that's just it. Another question that has escaped the guillotine… another question that cannot be satisfied by an answer of the mind. It's another question that's alive. What is this consciousness?"

Then Adam looked out the train windows and continued, "Maybe it's good to explore where we direct our consciousness, which only brings about other questions. Do we direct consciousness more outwardly or more inwardly? Do we direct it as a more focused beam or do we illuminate it? Or do we experiment with all these ways? Sometimes directing consciousness inwardly and sometimes outwardly… sometimes as a more focused beam and sometimes illuminating it…"

Collin, whose state of consciousness seemed more illuminated at that point, waited to respond. In that state he was simultaneously aware of the movements outside of himself as well as his own inner thoughts, feelings and bodily sensations. He even attended to the peripherals while his new thoughts formulated.

"I wonder," said Collin, "if I have the complete ability to direct consciousness at all. Sometimes it seems that I do while at other times it seems that I do not. I have noticed, as you say, that our conscious experience can be more or less illuminated and more or less focused. But I question if I really command this or if it just happens."

"Have you ever experimented with trying to direct consciousness?" asked Adam.

Then a series of memories entered Collin's presence; they were of a time when he had worked with other people in experiments related to conscious experience.

"Yes," Collin replied, "I was part of a spiritual work group a few years ago and we would carry out various exercises in that vein. We met once a week, sometimes twice, where we would carry out these different experiments. I still do some of them even to this day."

"What were the results?" inquired Adam.

Collin said, "Well, it seems to me that there are times when I appear to have the power to direct consciousness and then there are times I do not. For example, each morning I do a special exercise that directs consciousness to the body. I take a certain posture, I close my eyes and I move about the body sensing the whole. So during this exercise it seems that

I have the ability to do. In the morning I have the attention and ability to direct my conscious experience. But when I'm out in the world, as we both are right now, my conscious experience seems to 'just happen'. At one minute one thing catches my attention, the next minute another and so on. So while my attention is moving this way and that, I don't seem to have the ability to do. During those moments, I feel like a dog that's being walked by his owner. Meaning, I don't feel like I'm truly guiding my conscious experience. Overall, I think it's difficult to have command over anything consciously when all kinds of things attract us. Or maybe it's just more difficult?"

"It's no wonder that some of the monks in Tibet spend several years or even lifetimes meditating in caves," replied Adam. "Trying to escape the Maya… the Great Illusion…"

Collin said, "Really… I've considered the same kind of thing myself. I've thought about maybe heading off to the southwest and getting lost in nature. Living a more solitary life away from people…"

"What stops you?" asked Adam.

"I'm not sure," said Collin. "Sometimes it seems like fear stops me and at other times it seems that I still find value in working amongst people. There are certain precepts that I would not be able to practice if I lived in solitude."

"What kind of precepts?" asked Adam curiously.

"The work of not displaying negative emotions for one," said Collin. "If I didn't live amongst people, I wouldn't be able to practice this. I also couldn't work on things like developing patience, tolerance and love of kind. There is a benefit to treading the spiritual path in society."

Adam's face brightened up at that moment and he asked Collin if he was a Christian man. This question seemed so sincere and with such a childlike honesty that Collin couldn't help but feel moved by Adam's expression.

"You could say that I am an aspiring Christian," said Collin, "with the hope that I'll become a true Christian when I can live my life in complete harmony with Christ's teachings. I was raised a Catholic. I suppose I'll be a Christian when I discover how to love my enemy… when I can love God wholeheartedly and when I can turn the other cheek…"

"Have you ever made an effort to turn the other cheek?" Adam asked.

Then a whole series of violent images came into the mind's eye of Collin Hartley. He could see all of the fights he'd been in from early childhood all the way up until young adulthood. He saw fists flying, knuckles bloodied and shattered glass sticking out from lacerations in his own flesh. He also felt the anger and the desperation that came with those fights, and he felt ashamed that all of this was a part of his past.

"No," Collin replied, "I've always struck back. My pride was too strong and my drive to be a better human being was too weak. Then again, it has been many years since I have been in a fight with anyone. How about you?"

Adam looked down at the floor as if he were ashamed also and then responded, "I turned the other cheek once… A neighbor got mad at me for running my lawnmower a little too far into his yard (if you can believe that). Really, the whole thing was bizarre. He came running out of his garage and then cracked me right in the jaw. So I turned the lawnmower off and faced him. I didn't say a word… I just quietly gave him the opportunity to strike me again."

"What did he do?" asked Collin.

"He looked at me like I was crazy," said Adam, "and he told me to stay out of his yard. Then he went back into his garage. It was the strangest damn thing…"

Adam cleared his throat and continued, "And man, if I didn't feel proud of myself after that whole scene. I talked about it with everyone I knew. My wife, my brother, our priest and everyone in my Sunday church group… I really patted myself on the back for that one. But after a certain period of time, I started to feel ashamed. I felt shame for my sense of pride… shame for all my swaggering and shame for my holier than thou attitude. And it was then that I realized I had missed out on a golden opportunity.

"Turning the cheek is an individual discipline designed for personal transformation. I recognize that. Definitely not advisable for society at large. You still need to fight in protection of the vulnerable. Leaders take that sacred duty of defending their nation. For us on the Christian path, turning the cheek is a personal exercise. It is meant to help us love our enemy and to follow God's instruction that we can show love for Him by loving one another. It changes our relationship with God and it changes the Soul experience."

Collin, who was actively listening to Adam, continued feeding his heart through the simple love of being conscious. His observations seemed almost outside the body as he looked at himself and Adam carrying on a conversation. The subject of the talk didn't seem as important as the fact that these two guys were really sharing themselves with one another. These were not two contemporary men chatting in the Big City. These were two Souls huddled together in a Sweat Lodge having a transcendent exchange.

"I'm curious about the work that you do with the Sunday church group," said Collin.

Adam looked at him as if they had been friends for years and said, "We aspire to be Christians just like you, Collin. We know that anyone can call themself a Christian or a Catholic, yet to really be one is different. So, we support each other in working to be Christians. This week we're working with doing to others as we would have them do to us. The Golden Rule. This seems like an easy practice but it's proving to be a real challenge."

"What are your own personal challenges with this work?" asked Collin.

"I think there's one example that will explain this well," said Adam, "and it has to do with my brother. See, my brother was just recently divorced from his wife. They were married for five years before the divorce. My brother, who has major depression, will go through his cycles where he experiences extreme lows. I get frustrated with him. Really, I don't know how to help him. Maybe I don't always treat him with dignity and love. He refuses to meet with a doctor or therapist for treatment.

After five years of some pretty heavy down cycles his wife decided she did not want to be on that journey with him any more. Now my brother either calls me or comes over to my house looking for support. I love my brother, but I struggle with how to help him. I struggle with how to treat him as I would like to be treated in that situation. I struggle first because I've never felt depressed like him and I find it hard to relate, and second, because I just don't know the best thing to do for him. Sometimes I think I should use the tough love approach and strongly encourage him to seek out treatment, and other times I feel it's best to simply love him and let things work out at his own pace. The only problem is that he's prone to suicidal thoughts and I don't want him to end his life. So as it stands now I'm doing more of the tough love thing and pushing treatment. But again, I'm torn… do I continue pushing him into treatment or do I lay off and just be as comforting as possible? And just this one example shows that working to treat others as you would like to be treated is not so simple. There are internal conflicts that arise and no perfect solutions."

"Yes," Collin replied, "this internal conflict of ours… this struggle between our yes and no. Loving someone and wanting the best for someone does not always mean you have answers. Sometimes you feel like there's a whole community of different people living inside. All of them arguing with one another over every decision… the simple decisions as well as the tough decisions…"

Adam responded, "A Mr Gurdjieff once said that man's name is legion, and I believe this is the same kind of conclusion that you're suggesting. He says that man is a multiplicity and that he consists of hundreds of little men inside himself… often fighting over who will be in control. Fighting over what to do…"

Collin heard the call for the Chicago Avenue stop so he searched his thoughts for parting words.

"This is where I get off," he said, "and I wish you well in the work with your Sunday group, Adam. I hope your brother heals. I wish for your happiness. I wish you the best in your quest for transcendence."

They shook hands and Adam replied, "Those on the way converge and find one another, Collin. So I won't say goodbye to you… only see you later…"

Collin Hartley left the train and headed to work. On the way to work he stopped by to visit the homeless woman he saw praying the day earlier. He saw her from inside the coffee house where he sipped on his chai tea and watched the passers-by. She seemed so committed to her prayers and so heartfelt in this expression that Collin knew time spent in her presence would not be wasted. As he approached, he could see her sitting in a doorway of an abandoned building while she said her prayers. She had long gray hair and well-weathered skin that seemed like leather. She wore three layers of winter coats and her legs were covered in an old, dirty bed comforter. As he went nearer, he could hear the woman reciting 'The Lord's Prayer'. Quietly, over and over again:

Our Father who art in heaven,
hallowed be thy name,
thy kingdom come,
thy will be done,
on earth as it is in heaven.
Give us this day our daily bread.
And forgive us our trespasses,
as we forgive those who trespass against us.
And lead us not into temptation,
but deliver us from evil.

As Collin's shadow moved over the light of this woman's presence, she stopped praying and opened her eyes to look up at him.

With a toothless smile she said, "Sit down and join me… please…"

She patted the ground next to her and Collin took a seat.

"I saw you here yesterday," he said, "and now today we meet."

The woman nodded her head and replied, "It's good that you came today. By tomorrow my work here will be done."

"Where will you go next?" asked Collin.

"I'll be going to Lawndale next," she replied, "and then onto Englewood, then the Southshore, then Grant Park… and then I'll move around through Lincoln Park, Uptown, Rogers Park, Ravenswood and Logan Square. Then I'll come back here again."

"I'm curious about your work," said Collin, "and your prayers."

The woman put her hand on Collin's knee and responded, "It's all very simple really. I move about the city praying for all of the people. I love them… I wish God for them… so I pray for them…"

Then she crossed her hands and said, "Enough talk… if you want to stay, just pray with me."

Again, she closed her eyes and started reciting 'The Lord's Prayer', and Collin joined her, only he did not say the prayer aloud. This was between him and God, so the words and feelings associated with it remained unseen and unheard. After a half hour, Collin stood up and then headed off to work.

As he passed by all of the other cubicles at Restful Eternities, he could see his coworkers lying on the ground while they made their sales pitches. Some of the guys had their shoes kicked off, some turned their coats into pillows and had their heads buried in them, and a few had crawled underneath their desks. They all seemed very relaxed and almost complacent about their calls. The atmosphere in the office was very different, as even the tiniest trace of worry associated to sales had vanished. This brought a smile to Collin's face as he entered his own cubicle. Collin didn't have a minute to get situated before this entire mood shifted.

Tim seemed more tense than usual and he approached Collin's cubicle while shaking his finger and saying, "I knew that I should have gotten rid of you months ago, Collin! I should have sent you home when I first discovered that you were the moldy piece of bread in the bunch!"

Then Tim became even more animated and said, "Yeah, that moldy piece of bread that turns the whole loaf to shit if you don't catch it in time! Because of you, Collin, our sales are down twenty percent this quarter! Yeah, twenty percent because I forgot to throw away the rotten apple… the bad seed… the stinkin' moldy piece of bread! It's a known fact that in this business you cannot hold onto a caller that contaminates the whole group! You just can't do it… so I'm letting you go, Collin!"

And there it was, the closest thing that Collin Hartley had as an enemy in the world standing right before him. Collin felt the hurt, the frustration and the burning of his pride blazing away inside himself. However, he was aware enough not to project his feelings out towards Tim and he even took advantage of the moment by not displaying these negative feelings.

Collin asked calmly, "Should I leave today, Tim?"

"No," said Tim, who was obviously irritated by Collin's mere presence. "It's company policy to give you two weeks! This company has gone soft. I can't fire people same day any more. You all have rights now. You need to wrap everything up! So consider this day one!"

Tim paced around and searched for more words while Collin sat quietly. Collin wondered why the agency gave people two weeks' notice before termination. It was comical, ironic and added to the absurdity of the whole experience at Restful Eternities.

Then Tim continued, "You have to understand that the nature of this business is to make sales, Collin. And we give you all the freedom in the world to make that happen. At the end of the day if there's no money in the bank then there is no Restful Eternities. It's just that simple…"

Collin of course knew these points all too well. He really wasn't interested in sales and owing to this disinterest, he knew that the job would only last for so long. Needless to say, Collin was not surprised that he was being let go, nor was he shocked by the way Tim was treating him.

"So, just continue with the regular call lists," said Tim, "and then wrap everything up two weeks from today."

Then Tim walked away saying, "Damn moldy piece of bread… turning my whole loaf into shit…"

Collin reviewed his call list for the day but before he was able to get started, a coworker came to visit him. This was out of the ordinary since Collin had never really spoken with any of his coworkers in the past. Each cubicle at Restful Eternities is like an island to itself and the inhabitants of each island have no real means of communicating with one another. So there before Collin was a man who made the effort of paddling a boat over to his island. Collin, who was sitting on the floor cross-legged, looked up at him curiously.

The man said, "If you're interested… my cousin has a telemarketing business selling vacations to Costa Rica. I could get you in there if you want. It's actually pretty profitable and he's been doing well with it for over two years now."

Collin smiled at the man and said, "Thanks, but I'm actually considering another line of work altogether."

"What do you think you'll do?" the man asked.

"I'm not sure yet," said Collin. "I'm going to have to think it over."

The two of them became silent and then Collin quickly considered future job prospects. For years now he had the desire to do work that demanded more from him physically. He thought that maybe a carpentry job or a masonry job would be fitting. He remembered how much he valued physical work in his youth and he believed it would be a good future pursuit as well.

"I think I'd like to do something more labor intensive," said Collin. "Maybe woodworking… or maybe bricklaying… a job where I can use my hands more and my mouth less…."

The man snorted as he laughed and replied, "Oh, you want to move back down the working ladder."

"Are you sure this would be a move down the work ladder?" asked Collin.

"If you take calluses on your hands and back problems into consideration, then yes," the man responded.

Collin just smiled and then shook his head at his coworker. Again, the man offered him the referral to his cousin's place selling vacations, but Collin thanked him and politely declined. Finally, the man paddled back to his cubicle.

Collin Hartley turned his attention back to his calling list and decided he would try something altogether new. He decided to work against his usual habit of calling the people on the list in alphabetical order from A to Z. Instead, he opted to call people in the reverse order going from Z to A. And rather than holding the phone receiver with his right hand, he decided to hold it all day with the left. Collin thought this would be a good way to struggle with a habit and he believed that it would help him to Observe Anew.

He ran his right index finger through the Z list and then said aloud, "Okay, let's start with you, Mrs Zwibel."

Chapter Four: The Breakfast

Collin Hartley woke up. He placed one of his pillows over his face to block out the morning sunlight. He wanted a few more minutes of darkness; a few more minutes to stay inside himself. Collin felt calmed and free in that tranquil, nebulous state. It was like the deepest sleep where dreams don't even exist. He was lost in it, that is, he was lost in it until the crash of a garbage truck outside startled him. So Collin pulled the pillow off of his face and acquainted his dry eyes with his surroundings. The bedroom looked the same as the day before and Tarazina was standing in the doorway. Only today Collin did not call his cat over to his side. Instead, he looked up at the ceiling fan while it turned slowly around and around. He gazed up at it while the most obvious question came into his presence: what has disappeared today?

Before any other part of himself ventured to answer that question, Collin came to his feet and folded up his sheets. That question loomed in him but it seemed like he just ignored it. He started whistling the song 'Waiting for the Miracle', like he did the day before, only now he was not feeling cheerful. Collin felt even more tired and depressed while he creased and folded his sheets.

He managed to crack a smile and ruffle the top of Tarazina's head before he made it out of the bedroom. This took a special effort on his part since all he really wanted to do was get into the shower. His cat seemed happy as usual and she followed Collin with her eyes as he walked into the bathroom.

Collin urinated, he brushed his teeth and then he got into the cold shower. The water was freezing but this didn't seem to have much of an effect on him. Collin felt numb and void of any possible expression. He soaked, lathered and rinsed his body. He saw the dirt water swirl towards the drain which he thought was an adequate metaphor for his life.

As Collin dried off and headed towards the east room of his apartment, he felt the ache in his legs from sitting in unaccustomed positions the day before. He'd spent the entire previous day either standing or sitting cross-legged, and this had proved to have an effect on him. Collin's knees felt tender from the inside, his hamstrings a little tight and his ankles were cracking. However, Collin assumed his posture on the floor and he followed through with the morning exercise.

Afterwards, Collin went into the kitchen to prepare his breakfast. When he opened the cupboard where his beloved bagels were stored, he could see that they had vanished. In fact, all of his food had vanished. He searched the fridge, the pantry and all of the remaining cabinets, but the findings were all the same. All of Collin Hartley's food was gone.

He stood naked at the center of his kitchen while bombarded by thoughts. How long until I starve to death? Will I be forced to eat the walls? I wonder if this has happened to anybody else? Who is doing this to me? Is it a spiritual master? Is it God? Maybe I am creating this experience? Am I psychotic?

Then Collin thought to hell with the food, and he grabbed the teakettle. Collin went to the sink to fill it up, but the pipes were dry. So Collin took the teakettle to the bathroom sink where he was sure there was water, but there was now no water in there either. He was stumped by this since only minutes earlier, he brushed his teeth in this sink. Then Collin tried the shower, but it too was empty. The water was there a few moments ago but totally gone now. He found himself right at the point where the vanishing was happening.

Collin threw the teakettle down the hall and into the living room shouting, "Fine! Take it! Take it all! You don't make any sense to me… one minute you give me water and the next you take it away…"

And there he was, overtaken by anger and fear both at the same time. Collin would have also felt ashamed if he only noticed how ridiculous he looked standing naked in the bathroom while screaming at the air.

Then Collin took a seat on the toilet to collect himself, and it was at that moment he felt the shame of being overtaken by his anger and fear. He felt weak, disappointed and helpless. But at the same time Collin Hartley felt a sudden burst of confidence that he could make it through all of this. So he stood up and went on with his routine (only after checking the toilet for water which was bone dry).

Be as it May.

As Collin dressed himself, he told Tarazina that her food was gone and that there was no water in her bowl. He told her that he was sorry for this and that if she wanted to leave, he would harbor no ill feelings. The cat naturally looked up at him cluelessly while he tied his shoes and buttoned up his coat.

Then Collin headed out the door for work, all the while perplexed as to why he had water when he cleaned up, yet it was gone when he went to prepare breakfast. Then the 'why' vanished and he just felt happy that he was able to clean himself up at all that morning.

As Collin descended the stairs in his building, he saw Ms Weeks coming out of her apartment. She locked her door and greeted Collin with an enthusiastic smile.

"Good morning, Ms Weeks," Collin said in the most positive voice he could muster up.

Be happy and make others happy.

"Oh, Mr Collin," she said while caressing his shoulders, "how are you doing this morning?"

He thought for a second that he might share some of his experience with her but then he decided against it.

"I'm good," he replied, "I'm good."

"And the little kitty cat?" she inquired.

"Oh, Tarazina has it made up there," he said while looking in the direction of his apartment. "She gets a lot of love and attention…"

Ms Weeks replied, "And a lot of affection, I'm sure!"

Then as the two of them walked towards the front of the building she asked, "When are we going to have dinner again, Mr Collin? You know how I love to cook for you…"

"Anytime you'd like, Ms Weeks," he said while a curious thought came over him. Collin thought that this could be an interesting way to see if food materialized if he ate in her presence. He suspected that it would not, yet he felt it couldn't hurt to explore this possibility.

"Well, it's settled then," Ms Weeks replied. "Next Friday at my place. I will make a succulent vegetarian lasagna with homemade garlic bread… and we'll have baklava for dessert."

"That sounds delicious," said Collin while he held the front door open for her.

He wondered for a moment if Ms Weeks had food and water.

They stood on the sidewalk for a moment and before they departed, she said, "And my beautiful niece will be joining us, Mr Collin. She is a most precious young woman. I think you will like her very much!"

Be happy and make others happy.

Collin just smiled and thanked her for the invite, and then he headed towards the train. On the way, Collin considered seriously how the lack of food and water would affect him. He knew from past fasting experience that he'd be fine for the first day or two. It was the thought of day three and beyond that brought about the cold sweat.

Then Collin looked around and was struck by the simple yet perplexing fact that there was food and drink all around him. He saw the snow on the ground, the pine trees looming above and the patches of green grasses, all of which he knew could be consumed to nurture the body. What was perplexing was the idea that maybe he should refrain from consuming these eatables. One part of himself suggested that he trust his new perceptions and fast altogether while another part suggested that he boil the snow into water, turn the pine needles into tea and suck the juice out of the raw grasses. However, after this confrontation of thought, Collin concluded that he would wait to consume these things and only if he felt he was in real danger.

Be here now.

He arrived at the train platform where he became curious about a man who seemed to be eating his breakfast there. Collin got as close to him as he could without raising any suspicion. The man pretended to drink his coffee from an empty Starbucks cup and he chewed on a nothing that was supposed to be a scone. What was remarkable was that the cup was steaming even though it was empty, and the man's jaws really appeared to be stuffed with food. His hand even seemed to really be holding onto the scone.

The train pulled up and as always, Collin took it to the Belmont Avenue stop. The only difference was that on this day, the people were standing and many, like the man on the platform, were enjoying the nothings that they called breakfast. He saw people toss phantom donut holes into their mouths and he saw others sip on the refreshing void they believed was Mountain Dew. In a way, this scene made Collin hungry and thirsty, but he made do with the foods of air and impressions alone.

Collin exited the train at Belmont Avenue and walked into Renee's where the patrons sat on the ground and enjoyed their phantom breakfasts. Servers knelt down to pour the emptiness from their coffee pots into the void of each person's cup. The bus boys scrambled amongst the floor to pick up spotless dishes and gleaming silverware, and of course everyone carried on as if nothing were out of the ordinary.

Collin sat down across from Willie where he was eye level with the saltshaker on the bicycle. The seat was still there and the saltshaker was filled to the top with the familiar white crystals. Collin looked around at the saltshakers throughout the restaurant and all of them were empty. However, people still acted as if they were salting their food to their own personal liking.

Then Collin looked at Willie and noticed a change in him. It was hard for Collin to formulate just what this change was, but it seemed it was a change in his overall being. Willie looked at Collin with what appeared a subtle grin, but he seemed detached from his surroundings and unconcerned with what was happening in the restaurant. The Mysterious William Green was graceful in the way he looked about the room, all the while assuming his perfect lotus position.

"The food is gone," said Collin. "The food, the drink and even the salt… that is, all of the salt but yours, Willie."

Then Collin looked at the bicycle and ran his fingers over the middle frame saying, "This bike must be magical. It's unaltered in its alterations… it's unaffected by all of this…"

"Who do you think you are?" said Willie abruptly, yet at the same time dispassionately.

Willie's tone shocked Collin, since this was the first time he'd ever spoken to him in this way. His words were forceful, yet they were not belittling and hurtful. This woke Collin up a little and made him think seriously about the question.

Collin replied, "I'm a desperate man, Willie. I want… I wish for… and I long for something that I don't understand at all. Nothing satisfies… I thirst and I hunger, and I feel like I'm trying to pacify these things in the wrong way."

At that point a server came over and poured Collin a fresh cup of nothing and then she gave Willie a warm-up on his. The Mysterious William Green gave her a bright smile and then thanked her for the service.

Collin continued, "I go about my day practicing all of the things that have been taught to me. I do my morning exercise and my meditations… I work along my eight points and through this I try to wake up… to become conscious of the truth…"

Willie sipped his nothing and responded, "It's very easy to forget practicing 'Be As It May'. This is of course one of your eight points and like I said, it's very easy to forget practicing this. Think of the torture and struggles Upasani Maharaj endured. The King of Austerities. Unimaginable. To really have the 'Be As It May' attitude means 'To Be'. And that's what's most important for you, Collin Hartley… just 'To Be' present… in whatever life brings your way. Whatever will Be will Be."

Then Collin sensed himself; he sensed his body, his posture and his place in the restaurant. Then he thought maybe Willie was right since he could see that up until this point, he had in fact been lacking in being.

Before Collin spoke, he noticed something interesting in this return to being more self-present. He realized that although all food and drink had vanished from Renee's, the aroma of breakfast was still in the air. He smelt the home fries, the banana walnut pancakes and the spinach with feta cheese omelets. The fresh squeezed orange juice added its scent to the ensemble, and it was joined by the bouquets of coffee and tea. What's astonishing was that these smells fed an aspect of Collin that didn't seem to be fasting at all that day.

See The Spirit that moves in All Things.

"My expectations," said Collin, "they cause me more problems than anything else. I expect that since I exercise spiritual practices that I should have immediate spiritual results. I expect enlightenment and I expect God to be greeting me at the pearly gates. Buddha stressed this as the second point of his four noble truths. First, life is suffering. Second, it is our own desire and expectations that create the suffering."

Then Collin paused while he sipped his emptiness and continued, "I forget the most important things. I forget 'To Be'… I forget myself in the clutter of what I think I should be or in the imaginative visions of what I think I am. My desires and expectations take me out of the present moment."

Willie dawned a grin and said, "Well, don't go beating yourself up over these expectations. Remember, Collin… you have a life that's falling to pieces you must worry about. You want things to be different now. Even though this is exactly what you were asking for months ago. The desire to become desireless is the last desire."

Collin laughingly replied, "Yes, and I just lost my job to boot. Not that I ever really desired that job. First it was the bed, then the chairs, then the job and now it's food and drink. Although, I still have two weeks left at Restful Eternities. Very weird HR policy. Most places just fire you on the spot."

It was at that point when Collin returned to attending Willie's presence, and he still couldn't help but feel that there was something different about him. Again, it was his being alone that seemed different. Everything else was the same. Collin even thought for a moment that he might comment to Willie about this observation but then he decided that it would be inappropriate.

Collin said, "I know that I can quench my thirst by boiling down some snow and I know that I can eat raw grasses if my body gets emaciated. Maybe chew on a shred of inner bark. But I've made a promise to myself, that I will only consume these things if my life's in jeopardy."

"Have you ever fasted the body to the limits of its life force," asked Willie.

"No, I haven't," replied Collin. "I've only done twenty-four-hour fasts from food and drink. Although, I have experimented with longer fasts, but those were juice and fruit fasts. Those were three-day and five-day fasts."

"What did you notice during your twenty-four-hour fasts from the food and drink?" Willie inquired further.

"Well," said Collin, "I noticed an interesting duality take place where I experienced my physical body as diminishing yet I feel something else inside of me coming fuller to life. At times it even seems as if this inner something feeds off of the physical body. I'm drinking of my own blood and I am eating my own flesh."

"This is good that your food and drink has vanished," responded Willie. "You should take this fast as far as you can. It also sounds like you have a good plan for yourself. You should eat and drink only if it becomes absolutely necessary. Trust this process as it unfolds."

After Willie spoke, Collin realized that he had to use the bathroom, so he excused himself and headed towards the furthest corner of the restaurant. As he walked, he could feel the subtle faintness that comes with missing a meal. His mouth was also dry, and he licked his lips while passing through the bathroom door. Then Collin urinated and felt a little embarrassed since there was no water to flush his fluids. Luckily his urine drained naturally beneath. After this piss, Collin zipped up his pants and then walked over to the sink. He didn't even attempt to wash his hands. Instead, he looked at his image in the bathroom mirror. He seemed a little pale and he thought that it would be nice if he had some oil to rub over his head. However, he knew that there was nothing at his disposal that could bring the color back to his face, so he went out of the bathroom.

It was upon returning when Collin saw that the Mysterious William Green had left with his bicycle; Willie had vanished and in his place was a small glass bottle that contained a light blue liquid. Collin picked up the bottle and opened it. He took a whiff of the contents and the smell was wonderfully aromatic. Collin couldn't even describe the scent to himself.

Although, he felt that this perfume expressed the qualities of renewal and upliftment. Then he put a dab of this liquid in the palm of his left hand and rubbed it with the opposite thumb. It seemed to be an exotic oil of some kind. Collin, who remembered his wish for such an oil, splashed more into his hands and then lightly rubbed it over his face, the results of which were truly replenishing. Collin was so caught up in the experience that he failed to notice the server standing next to him.

She asked awkwardly, "Would you like a refill on your coffee?"

Collin fumbled to put the cap back on the bottle and said, "Oh, no thank you… I'm actually leaving."

He paid the server for the two cups of nothing and then headed downtown for work. He took the train to the Chicago Avenue stop and then walked directly to his building. Before Collin entered Restful Eternities, he looked up at the sign hanging above the doorway. He meditated on that sign, as he did many mornings, and he paid special attention to the engraving of the full moon as it rose above the words Restful Eternities. It seemed that the moon looked down on those words in the same way it looks down on people at night. It was as if it were hungry and seeking the best morsels to feed its appetite on.

Then Collin felt a wave of terror come over himself as he believed that the moon turned its attention directly towards him. At that point, the moon started to grow and as it got bigger, it burst out of the limitations of the sign.

Then it grew even larger than Collin and all he could do was stand paralyzed in one spot. He felt that death was close and he knew there was no escaping it. But then the moon halted, it stopped its advance and it even appeared to give Collin one chance at fleeing. Collin moved his eyes about in search of a direction to run, but there was nowhere for him to go. And just when everything seemed hopeless, just when it seemed Collin would be devoured for certain, he made a sudden leap inside. Yes, Collin Hartley dove inside himself.

He was quick off the line and he bolted straight inside with the speed of a cheetah. And the only thing that stopped him from a clean getaway was the fact that this fast redirection inwards turned him inside/out. So, in this action, Collin Hartley really went nowhere. However, this getting turned inside/out sobered him from this daydream and the moon returned back to its normal position on the sign.

Collin Hartley looked down at his body and continued standing in front of the sign for a few more minutes. This experience of getting turned inside/out was cleansing yet at the same time it depleted him of energy. He felt tired in his physical self but uplifted internally. In a way he felt that this action had set him right.

Lord Avatar Meher Baba. King of Kings.

Collin ascended the stairs to the second floor and his body felt heavier than normal, even wearisome. Each step was like a super effort and at one point he wasn't sure that he could go on at all. But Collin remained disciplined and he exerted all that he had so that he could make it to the top. And when he finally reached the calling floor, Collin truly felt accomplished.

When he entered the main calling area, he could see that everything was different. The dry erase board had smiley faces and lightning bolts drawn on it rather than the usual calling statistics and quarterly earnings figures. He saw paper airplanes strewn about the floor as if a great battle in the sky had taken place earlier. As he walked towards his cubicle, he heard coworkers talking to themselves rather than making sales pitches by phone. He even heard weeping and moaning from some of these men. This sparked Collin's curiosity and he observed attentively as he headed towards his cube. When he ventured further down the center aisle, he heard one man crying from inside his cube, and when Collin neared him, the man said, "I can't believe this is my life! I'm invading the homes of the innocent like a snake!"

Collin remained silent as he could not think of anything to say.

Then the man buried his face into his hands and continued, "I'm selling these people their own death! I make money off this prostitution of death! I am a money whore of death!"

Collin stood there while the pity, guilt and empathy came over him. He felt pity because of this man's helpless state, and he felt guilt owing to the fact that he too sold death to people by phone. And these two taken together drew out his empathy since Collin knew that they were not all that different. They both lived pathetic lives and the feeling of this was expressed perfectly by the man Collin Hartley looked upon. And before he had a chance to speak with this coworker, Collin heard the voice of someone else behind him.

Collin turned to find another coworker clenching his fists and belting out, "If I can manage just two sales a week, I'll be able to afford the new car and the new set of golf clubs!"

Collin staggered towards this other man, who was sitting on the floor, and Collin supported his weight by holding onto the outer wall of this man's cubicle. This guy was sprawled out on the ground and he was surrounded by several pictures of cars and golf clubs. These images encircled him while he continued with his verbalized thoughts.

"It will only take four weeks with two sales each week! This will be easy! And let's see... I make between two hundred to three hundred calls each day so that's an average of twelve hundred to thirteen hundred calls each week..."

Then the man grinned from ear to ear while picking up two pictures; one was of a silver Acura and the other was a set of Calloway golf clubs, and he said, "You're as good as mine, my precious beauties... you're as good as mine!"

Collin turned away from this man and then headed further in the direction of his own cubicle. On the way he caught a glimpse of the man who had paddled over to his cube the day earlier.

This coworker stood at the center of his cubicle like a Libra; he moved his hands up and down like the scales of Lady Justice and asked, "Should I stay here or should I go to work for my cousin? Should I sell grave plots or should I sell vacations to Costa Rica? Should it be death or should it be life?"

Finally, Collin broke his silence by telling this coworker to choose life. And this statement startled the man who then replied, "Oh yes, I think I would prefer selling vacations to Costa Rica also."

Then this man outreached his hand to Collin and said, "I'm Allen."

Collin shook his hand and introduced himself as well.

"So, this makes you the second person who knows my name here," Allen said. "Tim, of course, is the first…"

Collin asked, "Why is it that we don't know each other here? Why do we work together as strangers?"

"Well, for one thing," replied Allen, "knowing each other is not good for sales. I mean… if everyone here were friends, we wouldn't get any work done."

Collin smiled and asked, "Is that you talking or is that Tim talking?"

Allen chuckled and said, "I guess that's Tim talking. But hey… someone's gotta talk for him today… you know, since he isn't here."

Collin grinned as he felt relieved from Allen's statement. He was happy that there would be no chastising, no verbal flogging and no being looked down upon.

"Yeah," said Allen, "our phone lines are dead today. No Internet. No phone. Tim even had a little breakdown… he told everyone to go home."

Then Collin looked around the calling floor; he saw two paper airplanes soaring high above the cubicles and he saw someone drawing a picture of the Willis Tower on the dry erase board.

"And yet nobody leaves," said Collin.

Allen looked around while shaking his head and replied, "I believe that this is home for those of us who've stayed. At least I know this is home for me anyway. When I think about my life… what home really is… I think about work. So Restful Eternities is my home. It is my life… for now anyway…"

Then Allen looked at Collin and asked him sincerely, "Isn't this home for you?"

Collin responded, "It's rare that I ever feel at home. I have moments… just seconds maybe when I feel at home. I think home is a state of mind."

Allen, who seemed confused by Collin's choice of words, said, "Well, maybe you can build your own home. Didn't you tell me yesterday that you wanted to do more work with your hands? You said you wanted to do something more labor intensive if I remember correctly. And what could be better than building your own house?"

"That's a great suggestion," said Collin. "Maybe you're right. Better to build our own home."

Allen stood there nodding his head as if he were very pleased with his contribution. Then he seemed to search for more words but there was nothing.

Collin said, "Well, Allen, I'm gonna head over to my cube and sort some things out. It was good talking with you."

When Collin turned to walk away, he experienced the same fatigue and heaviness that he felt on the stairs earlier. The first few steps took incredible effort and he had to struggle with not only his body's unwillingness to push forward, but also his fear that he might drop his carcass altogether. Collin thought this was strange since his body felt like it had been fasting for a week rather than a half day, but he took his position for what it was worth and then shoved on.

Allen followed Collin to his cubicle and asked, "So really, have you decided on the type of work you'll be doing when you leave here?"

Collin entered into his cube and thought for a moment about sharing some of his inner experiences with Allen. He considered telling Allen about his exercises, his eight points and the life that was vanishing before his very eyes. But Collin decided against this and instead spoke to Allen through allegories.

Collin looked around the office as if he were about to tell Allen a secret and then said, "Actually, I have already started building a home."

Allen, who couldn't hide his surprise, asked, "Where do you find the time to work on this home? And how do you cover the cost?"

Collin replied, "I work as often as I'm able to work, and the cost is covered by some investments I made, years ago. See, when my dad passed away, he left me an inheritance and I invested some of this into some stocks that ended up doing well. So, I used some of this money to purchase the land and the resources needed for building this home."

Allen's facial expression turned to compassion and he said, "Oh man, I'm sorry about your dad. He must have been young… I mean, you're so young yourself…"

Collin responded tenderly, "Yes, he did pass away young. He was a good man… a good father…"

The two remained silent for a moment and then Collin continued.

"I began building on this land a few years ago. I started by purchasing all of the necessary tools and I also bought a good solid building plan. Then I went fast to work… I jumped right in… And slowly but surely, I've been making something out of nothing. One brick at a time… learning and applying the new knowledge I acquire along the way."

"Man," said Allen, "that seems like a lot of work. Do you have anyone to help you?"

Collin grinned and then responded, "Well, the man who created the blueprint has been an enormous help. I never met him myself, but the building plan sure says a lot about him as a person. I mean, this man didn't miss a single detail. I was even given a handbook that corresponds to the blueprint. It's a step-by-step guide that takes you through the constructive process. He's even idiot-proofed it in some ways by pointing out potential dangers that come about while you're building."

Allen asked, "So do you have anyone that helps you with the actual labor? You know… do you have anyone that helps with the hammering, the sawing, the bricklaying and stuff like that?"

And it was then that the image of the Mysterious William Green appeared in Collin's mind.

"Yes," said Collin, "I do have someone that helps with the hands-on construction. He's well trained and has spent a lot of years in the construction business. I wouldn't have been able to come this far along without him. He's really a master builder and he doesn't miss a beat. He's hardworking, insightful and he, like the man who developed the blueprint, has the innate ability to spot potential dangers."

"So how much more do you have left to build?" asked Allen.

"That's hard to say," said Collin. "In many ways it seems that I could be working on this house for eternity. I'm always finding new things to work on... new projects that need attending..."

"So where exactly is this house being built?" Allen inquired further.

"Actually," replied Collin, "it's a lot closer than you might think."

"Wow," responded Allen, "it must have cost you a fortune to build around here!"

"Yes," said Collin, "in the end it will have cost me everything."

Then Allen really perked up and he asked Collin if he could visit the worksite. He seemed genuinely interested in Collin's home and it was obvious that Allen wanted to see it with his own eyes.

Collin looked at Allen and replied hesitantly, "Oh, I don't know, Allen. You see... I'm sort of self-conscious about who I show this house to."

"I understand," said Allen. "You want it completed to perfection before you show it off. I understand completely..."

Then Allen became more thoughtful and said, "I think it's great that you've found something you really believe in, Collin. I can tell by the way you talk about building your home that you love it. It's great to be doing work that has meaning for you… rather than just working to get by."

Collin took a seat on the ground and rested his back against the far wall of his cubicle. Then he signaled Allen to take a load off as well. They both got comfortable and then Collin responded to Allen's comments.

"It is important to find work that has meaning for you, but there's certainly no shame in working to 'get by' either. It can take years or even a lifetime to find work that's valuable. In the meantime, you have to survive and pay the bills. So, getting by with a job that only has a monetary value still serves a purpose. It can be a way to love others. A way to love and provide for your family. It can also offer peace of mind. I mean if you don't have a secure income, you might be in a constant state of worry or panic."

Allen tilted his head downward and started running his fingers over the carpet saying, "That's true, but it's still hard to figure out the type of work that has real meaning for you. Or I should say that it's hard for me personally to figure out what it is I really want to do in life. Sometimes I think about going to art school. I've always loved classical painting. You know like the paintings of Da Vinci, David and El Greco. The only problem is that I can't paint a lick…"

"Isn't that the reason you go to school?" asked Collin. "To get instructed and to develop your abilities with the guidance of a teacher?"

"You're right," replied Allen who seemed a little disappointed. "The only problem is that I question the type of teachers that are out there."

"What do you mean?" asked Collin.

Allen said, "Well, I've taken three different painting classes over the years and all have turned out the same results. All of the teachers I've studied under have helped me very little in my developing as a painter. See, all of these instructors are trained in expressionism, minimalism, post-modernism, conceptualism and so on… and I have no interest in learning those styles. I want to learn how to paint in a more traditional sense, and all of the teachers I've had in the past have only taught me what I already know. That is… they've helped me to relearn the way I sling colors onto a canvas."

Then Allen paused and thought for a moment. He searched for the right words and continued, "Of course, I did learn how to become a better bullshitter during critiques. You know… learning how to talk for an hour about what my mess of colors really means."

Collin grinned and then asked, "Have you ever thought about seeking out a teacher that will suit your needs? Have you considered visiting classes and talking with teachers before you sign up for their instruction?"

"No," said Allen, "that would make too much sense."

Collin started laughing and Allen continued, "Seriously! In a way I'm really lazy so I find it hard to apply common sense. I also like to fancy myself a victim so that doesn't help either. Tortured artist type. But you're right… of course, it would be better if I sought a teacher that could best train me in classical painting. Again… this would make too much sense."

While Collin laughed, he could feel a distinct change in his bodily sensations. He still felt fatigued and wearisome, but the laughter freshened up his state. Collin experienced a surge of upliftment and this was expressed to Allen when he spoke.

"What if I told you, Allen, that I know of a painting school that could suit your interests?"

Allen's eyes widened as he asked Collin, "Do you know of a school that teaches classical painting?"

Then in a flash, Allen's facial expression changed drastically; his eyelids suddenly dropped while his head tilted downwards and he said, "I bet it costs a fortune… and I bet they also want to see a spectacular portfolio… and I bet they expect a collection of wonderful paintings that I don't have…"

Then Allen looked at Collin, while he really continued the conversation by himself, and said, "Why do great art schools expect incredible works from you before you even get instructed? I mean… that's why you're applying to the school in the first place. You're applying so that you can become a great artist. So why do they want all this great art from you in advance?"

Collin replied jokingly, "Allen, you've turned yourself down for acceptance and you haven't even applied yet."

"I'm sorry," said Allen. "I do that all of the time. Like I said before, I fancy myself a victim sometimes. Anyway, please tell me about the school."

Collin explained, "The school is located in Lincoln Square and it's called Through Painting We Have MET. And MET is an acronym for Movements, Emotions and Thoughts. So, it's Through Painting We Have Movements, Emotions and Thoughts. These classes are taught by a couple, Mel and Nancy Leimer, and they can help you to develop this classical style you're talking about."

"Through Painting We Have MET," said Allen. "That sounds interesting. Existential. Have you ever visited the school yourself? When are the classes? Is it affiliated with any local universities?"

Collin expounded, "I can tell you some basics about the school and the instruction, but the rest will be up to you. First of all, the class day that you'd be eligible for is on Saturday mornings. The time of instruction is from nine in the morning till two in the afternoon. Each class begins with a group discussion where the work for that day is explained. And each class focuses on exploring one of the three aspects of a person: the bodily movements, the emotions or the thoughts. For example, a class that will be studying bodily movements for the day will happen like this: the teachers, Mel and Nancy, will pick a physical activity… it could be bouncing a basketball, mixing paint or washing brushes. Then, before actually doing any drawing or painting, each student will participate in the activity (and let's use bouncing a basketball, for example). Each student goes to the center of the classroom, one at a time, and starts dribbling the basketball. They pay special attention to the movements of their own body and the action of the dribbling. In short, they sense with their own body what it is like to bounce the basketball. Not as they remember it… not as they think it is… but how it is really sensed by the body in the NOW. And it's only after each student has had a turn bouncing the basketball that they stand before their easels ready to draw and paint (of course, there are models who will continue bouncing the basketballs while the students draw and paint them).

"The point here is that the students draw the models while keeping the dribbling action fresh in the memory of their own bodies. The challenge is to not only render what the bouncing action looks like, but to communicate what the sensations are like also. And I must say, Mel and Nancy are experts at helping you to develop technique and style in the way you render these actions."

Allen looked at Collin with childlike curiosity and asked, "So what about the classes where emotions and thoughts are explored?"

Collin said, "The classes that focus on the emotions and thoughts are the most celebrated. I once took part in a specific study on sorrow at the school and the results were astounding. Mel brought in a friend who plays piano and this guy was truly gifted. He played this piece that could have brought tears to the eyes of a snake. Really, it was an amazing piece of music. So, he performed this song that expressed sorrow, and then we students took turns sitting next to the piano player and humming along with his melody. The aim was for each one of us to feel this same sorrow reverberate throughout our self. And we did... we each felt the weeping of this song play in us. So, after we each took a turn, we went to our easels and then began our rendering. As with the study of movements, the goal was not to just draw this man playing the piano, but to communicate the sorrow as well. And, of course, Mel and Nancy go around from student to student to helping each to develop technique and style."

"So, what about the classes on thoughts?" Allen asked eagerly. "Tell me about the study of thoughts."

"The exploration of thoughts and ideas is the most meticulous work done at this school and owing to its very nature, I can only say a little about it. You really have to become involved yourself and experience these things first hand to have a clear understanding. Anyway, the study of thoughts involves taking certain questions or ideas and developing them into pictographs. This includes the use of symbols, character metaphors and icons. In these classes, the students take turns coming to the center of the classroom and expounding on certain questions or ideas. Then each student shares his or her opinion about how this question or idea can be represented visually. Each class on thoughts deals with one shared question or idea, so the student body in entirety will render a pictograph of the same thing. However, each may represent this question or idea in the manner in which they choose. And this is really all that I can say about the study of thoughts at this school."

The two turned quiet and Allen stared off into space as if a new world had opened up for him. It was like he was just beginning to see the lines of a majestic rendering that he had been overlooking his whole life.

He asked Collin, "How many weeks do the classes run?"

"Twelve weeks altogether," replied Collin. "It's three weeks of movements, three weeks of emotions and three weeks of thoughts with one critique week in between each grouping. So, you have your first three weeks in the study of movements with a following week dedicated to critique. Then three weeks in emotions… then critique… then three weeks of thought… then a final critique."

Allen asked, "What are Mel and Nancy like? How long has the school been around? Are there other schools like this?"

Collin wrote down their phone number on a piece of paper and handed it to him. "Give them a call," he said, "and go check it out before you sign up for classes.

Make sure this is the type of school that you want to attend."

Allen, who was visibly enthused, stood up and said, "Thank you, Collin... I'm gonna call as soon as I get back to my apartment tonight."

"Well, I wish you the best, Allen," said Collin. "I hope you find the type of painting teacher that you're looking for. I hear that they're hard to come by these days."

Allen just nodded his head in gratitude and then disappeared from Collin's sight. Through their conversation they have MET.

Chapter Five: Transportation

Collin Hartley woke up. His mouth was dry and his stomach grumbled, pleading "feed me" and "give me water". His body ached and felt more like a corpse than a living being. He opened his eyes and the first impression he received was of the atmosphere devouring him. Dust returning to dust. Then he experienced that he was devouring himself. He was partaking of his own bread and wine. His conscious observance was melting away the bodily sensations in its own mouth. His conscious experience even ate the thought, "what is happening to me", and then nibbled on his own inner weeping for dessert. It was then that his essence had breakfast. This meal filled its tum and gave it the proper nutrition to fuel for the beginning of the day. Collin was waking up and orienting himself to the Realm of False Light.

Collin burst out of his cotton sheets and staggered some while he began folding them into perfect formation. He was refreshed and alive internally, but his flesh was still depleted and wearisome. It seemed to Collin that his inner man was animating the corpse while it piled up the sheets and fluffed pillows. This made him feel truly dead and yet truly alive both at the same time.

Then Collin noticed Tarazina lying in the doorway of the bedroom. She seemed as tired and groggy as Collin's own flesh, but she still purred away when he started petting her. Love was not lost.

Collin asked, "What has vanished for us today, my love? Is it the lamps? Will it be the roads? Maybe it's the phones?"

Collin peeked out into his living room and saw that his lamps were still there and continued, "No, it's not the lamps…"

Then he stood up and walked towards the bathroom to prepare for the day. He wondered if 'the powers that be' would give him shower water as they did the day before. Collin received his answer when he turned all of the knobs in the bathroom and discovered that everything was dry. Then he stood in front of the toilet and tried to urinate, but there wasn't a drop. So Collin put the lid down and wondered what purpose he had being in the bathroom at all. It was then that a spontaneous idea came to him.

Collin Hartley walked out onto his back porch, half naked, and started rubbing himself down with snow. He focused on saturating all of the important parts. He first worked the snow all over his face, and then his genitals and up towards the armpits. Then he rubbed snow into his navel and finally his anus. Collin's feet were naturally cleansed by the snow since it was up past his ankles, so he didn't make any special effort in that direction. When he finished his snow bath, Collin went back into the apartment to dry off. He could have taken some of that snow into his mouth for refreshment. Instead, he relished in denying that same act.

Collin took a towel to his body and then looked at himself in the bathroom mirror. He was stunned to find that his complexion seemed clearer and that his teeth seemed whiter. Even his ratty beard seemed better groomed and his overall appearance was healthier. All of this was bizarre to Collin since he felt that his body was rotting away. It was weird for him to see an image of perfect health while at the same time experiencing this same image dying.

Afterwards, Collin went back into his bedroom to fetch the oil Willie had left for him the day before. He pulled the vial out from his coat pocket and looked at it. The faint blue hue was hypnotizing and it reminded him of a precious gem that had been altered into a liquid form. Then he took off the cap and whiffed the fragrance. It too was subtle yet at the same time powerful and uplifting. Collin put some of the oil in his hands and splashed it onto his face. He even applied some of it to his underarms and his navel. Then Collin put the cap back on the bottle, he kissed it and then put it away.

Collin dressed himself and then went to the east room of his apartment to complete his morning meditation exercise. He assumed the cross-legged position on the ground and began creating a true symmetry of the body. He was relaxed yet completely vertical and balanced all around. He turned his attention towards his breathing without altering it in any way. Collin closed his eyes and started moving his consciousness about the whole. He experienced a vast world inside and his attention moved through everything freely. In some places he was very dark and in other places very light. He moved deeper inside himself feeling as though he was spelunking through a cave that stayed naturally motionless and almost inviting each step of his expedition. Collin Hartley's consciousness traveled through tunnels, it climbed walls and at times was lost in a world of echoes. Then suddenly he opened his eyes; the exploration was over, and Collin left the room.

Collin considered skipping work for the day while he put on his socks and tied his shoes. He thought about going out to investigate whether or not Lake Michigan contained any water. He thought about calling Tim at work and telling him he was sick. Then Collin thought maybe the phone lines were down again and he wouldn't even have to make the call into the office. Then Collin drifted into a daydream and saw himself playing hooky down at North Avenue beach. He envisioned a massive lakebed without water in it and he saw himself running out towards the middle of it. But then he came back to his senses; he finished tying his shoes and decided to go about his day as usual.

It was upon leaving the apartment that Collin became aware of the vital disappearing of the day. He saw that all of the cars, trucks and city buses had vanished. He stood in front of his apartment building and watched as people ran up and down the street as if operating and riding vehicles. Collin saw one lady sprinting westbound while she pretended to steer her invisible car with her left hand and changing the radio station with her right hand. Then Collin observed this woman run past two men who acted like they were parking their phantom cars. These men seemed cautious while they turned their ghost wheels and stretched their necks out of nonexistent windows.

As Collin started walking towards the train, he even saw one man working on an invisible car in the alleyway next to his apartment building. The man cussed and mumbled obscenities while he took a wrench to phantom nuts and bolts. When Collin turned back towards the street, he saw a group of people running together as if they were passengers on a city bus. A driver, in full uniform, called out the Irving Park stop and then a few of them departed from the group. Some of the passengers that remained with the pack even scrolled through their iPads while others pretended to nap. This seemed comical to Collin as they all started moving their feet again. Those that napped moved their legs rapidly while their eyes stayed closed and heads tilted up against invisible windows. Others were on their iPads scrolling and tapping away as they sprinted onwards down the street.

Collin Hartley was simply amazed by all of this, and he just smiled as the people ran this way and that. The sounds of heavy machinery were now replaced with the footsteps of the people who owned these streets. He was so captivated by this scene that he almost got hit by a man driving an invisible car while he crossed the street.

Collin turned suddenly and a driver yelled, "Dude! Watch where the hell you're walking!"

Collin bowed his head apologetically and then the man sped off with his feet pounding the pavement, saying, "You're lucky you didn't get killed!"

When Collin finally reached the train station, he had to make a special effort to get up the stairs to the platform. The walk sapped physical energy that he could not spare, so he collected himself for a moment before making the ascension. He felt something charge up inside himself and then Collin's inner man pushed the outer man up the stairs effortlessly all the way to the top.

Collin reached the train platform and he smiled as a new series of fresh impressions came to him. He saw groups of people running up and down the train tracks as if they were passengers in separate cars. He looked to the north where one group vanished into the horizon; and then another group stopped in front of him to head southbound towards the loop. Collin stood there for a moment while the mass of people halted before him. He saw that everyone was standing, some pretending to eat breakfast while others napped and read newspapers. Then Collin leapt onto the tracks with the group and away they all went.

Collin felt like a child again as he raced with his fellow passengers towards downtown. It amazed him that this group could move their legs so fast yet carry on with their upper bodies as if they were standing in one spot. He saw one man with his head down and his arms crossed while his legs moved like a lizard across desert sand. But Collin did not try faking anything at all with his own upper body; instead, he moved his arms around briskly as if he were an Olympic runner going for the gold. This prompted some queer looks from his fellow passengers, but Collin thought nothing of it. He just moved his legs like a little league baseball player who was rounding third and heading home. All the while, Collin's body was putting up the red flags, screaming, "Danger! Danger! This body will drop if you keep pushing it like this!" But Collin paid no mind to these things either. Collin's inner man was tasting ecstasy and nothing could take that away from him; not even the death of his physical body.

When the group reached Belmont Avenue, Collin Hartley departed, and it was only then that he gave his physical body time to catch its breath. He leaned himself up against an advertisement while he panted and perspired. Collin's head was down as his eyes followed a bead of sweat that fell from his forehead and crashed onto the ground below. Collin thought, "I'm not sure if I can afford to lose any water right now," and then he began running his hands feverishly about his head; it seemed that he was trying to push the moisture back into his flesh.

After he caught his breath, Collin descended from the train platform and walked in the direction of Renee's Restaurant. It was then that he noticed the bike racks were empty and that there were no bike riders on the streets at all. He only saw people pretending to drive cars and ride buses. This seeming disappearance of bicycles of course made him curious as to whether or not Willie's bike had gone missing. However, Collin Hartley presumed that it had not.

This presumption proved true when Collin entered the restaurant and saw the Mysterious William Green sitting next to it while he sipped on his nothing. Willie was in the lotus position with his cup of emptiness while the shadow of his bicycle covered his body. Collin walked in between all of the patrons at Renee's while they chewed on their toasty nothings and sipped on their fresh empty beverages. Then he took his usual seat across from the Mysterious William Green.

"Thank you for the oil," said Collin as he positioned himself on the floor. "I don't think I've ever smelt something so fragrant and uplifting."

Willie just smiled and nodded his head as if to say "you're welcome".

Then Collin glanced at the bicycle; and then back at Willie saying, "I thought this bike would still be here…"

Willie took another sip of his nothing and looked at Collin as if he were indifferent to his comments.

It was at that moment when Collin realized a subtle glow about Willie; he seemed semi-transparent and he was emitting light. Collin searched into Willie's crystalline eyes and saw a clear reflection of himself in those glass-like orbs. Willie was poised in his translucency, and he almost appeared majestic to Collin Hartley. Then the Mysterious William Green spoke to him.

"I see that you're tending the corpse rather well, Collin Hartley."

"I really am dying," said Collin. "I really feel death working on me. My whole body, aches for water… for food… my mouth is dry, my flesh is turning cold and it feels like I've been fasting for two weeks rather than two days."

"And yet you are feeling very much alive," responded Willie.

"You're right," said Collin. "I don't know if I've ever experienced anything like this before. There's something in me that is elated… ecstatic at times… Meher Baba talked about spiritual suffering simultaneously offering subtle joy… the happiness of the aspirant…"

Willie grinned and said, "This is the Real You waking up. Keep paying attention to it and keep waking up."

Then Collin felt a sudden rush of fear come over his physical body and he toiled in inner panic. He felt that he was going to die in an instant and that the Real Self Willie referred to, would be tossed into oblivion.

The Mysterious William Green clapped his hands loudly and said, "I told you to wake up! And here you are drifting off into nightmares!"

Collin immediately returned to his center of gravity and the fear vanished. His imagination ran away in the light of Willie's hand clap and it was replaced with more objectivity.

Willie said, "You have to keep your Now Point present while the clock tic tocks, tic tocks. Stay present even during the excruciating pains and you'll make it."

Collin, who believed he was now being sincere with himself, replied, "At times I have doubts that I will make it, Willie. Sometimes I doubt if I can take this journey to the end."

"Then to hell with you," Willie said sharply. "If you work for the Highest you have to pay the Highest price! You have to experience the Highest sufferings and you have to make the Highest sacrifices!"

Willie's words shocked Collin, but they also gave him an unexpected feeling of self-confidence. They even slaughtered Collin's doubts and annihilated all remaining tinges of fear.

Willie continued, "You will continue dying and you will continue living. You will continue seeing this life for what it's for and you will continue waking up. You will disappear in one way and you will be found in another. You will also continue through great suffering and at the same time through great joy."

"You're not alone, Collin Hartley. You have all the Love, all the attention, and all support of the Divine."

Collin took a moment before he responded so that Willie's words could be totally absorbed into his self. On the surface, Willie's comments were dualistic, but a deeper part of Collin Hartley understood them quite differently. This inner man understood The Only of Willie's expression.

A server knelt down to pour Collin a fresh cup of nothing, and it was then that he asked the Mysterious William Green what it is like to completely Wake Up.

"To realize Oneself," replied Willie, "cannot be described through words. If you have not realized your True Self you cannot even imagine what it is like. It's beyond reason and beyond the comprehension of the human mind. To realize your True Self is beautiful beyond description so it cannot be limited by a description. The Real is above the false. This is all just a shadow of that Truth."

Then Willie thanked the server, who seemed curious about their conversation, and continued, "The Self Realization that results from the experience of human suffering is the goal of all life. And God shows you infinite love and infinite forgiveness during the stages of this Self Discovery. You of course can go nowhere without God. In fact, the more you truly love God the more you will migrate towards Him. And the closer towards this communion with God the more your weaknesses, fears and all other imperfections will get drawn out and destroyed. Your imperfections, of course, have to be annihilated… overcome… and completely abolished… the limited self must go…"

"Is there a way to expedite the process?" asked Collin.

Willie grinned and replied, "A few minutes ago you had doubts that you could go on at all. So how is it that you ask about expediting the process now? I thought you were giving up?"

"I don't know," said Collin. "I guess that I want to get there as quickly as I can. I think I just want it to end. I want to be done with this, Willie."

Willie looked at Collin lovingly. "It's God that graces you, it's God that cleanses you and it's God that takes away all that is unnecessary. It's God's mercy that allows you to approach Him and it's God's love that awakens you. The Great Awakener has come. The Compassionate Father welcomes you."

Collin became a little irritated and struggled not to show this irritation to Willie. He felt the static move about his body, but he kept it contained. And instead of exhibiting this irritation, Collin asked Willie a question.

"Is there a way that I can do something? Can I do anything at all?"

The Mysterious William Green pierced Collin Hartley with a spear-like gaze and then related a parable to him.

"An apple falls from a tree and onto the earth below. The apple remains in the shadow of the tree for a period of time, but then it's eventually consumed by the earth. This apple disintegrates into the dirt where it begins to rot and wither away. As the apple decays, the seeds partake of this nutrient and then sprouts grow out from the seeds. Then these sprouts eventually move up from underneath. After the sprouts break out of the ground they continue growing up towards the sun. And over time this same apple gets transformed into an apple tree."

Willie paused for a moment while he sipped his nothing and continued, "Now, from the apple's perspective, it would seem that it is 'doing' all of this since it bears witness to the entire process. The apple falls, the apple decays into the earth, the seeds of the apple sprout and then what's latent in the apple seed becomes realized. So, this apple becomes an apple tree. However, this whole process, as we both know, has nothing to do with any real 'choice' coming from the apple itself."

This parable had a somewhat humorous effect on Collin Hartley. He even envisioned himself as the apple in a comical reenactment of the parable. Collin saw himself as this apple just getting to fall from the branch. Literally, his face on the apple. He heard the stem breaking away from the tree and his apple-self exclaimed, "Okay, I've decided that I'm going to fall to the ground now!" Then he saw his apple-self plop into some mud where the earth opened its mouth and prepared to devour him. Then he said, "Okay, I've decided that I'm venturing into the earth now! I'm going to be brave and go where no apple has gone before!" So, the dirt swallowed him and over time his 'sweetness' rotted away in the earth's belly. Then Collin's apple-self began sprouting and he heard himself say, "Look at me growing! Nothing can stand in my way! Soon I will be all grown up!" Finally, Collin saw himself as a full-grown apple tree, smiling by all that he had accomplished through the apple ego.

After this daydream, Willie looked compassionately at Collin and said, "All that's required of you is to BE. Just BE, Collin… Just BE the apple as it transforms into the apple tree. Bear witness to the miraculous."

At that point, all traces of Collin's internal comedic play disappeared and for a moment he experienced a sense of being that was completely new to him. His thoughts were stilled, his emotions tamed and his presence saturated with something that he could never explain. Collin could not even formulate a new thought so he sat there silently.

Willie, almost whispering, said, "Remember yourself… remember that you are waking up… The Divine is waking up through you…"

The Mysterious William Green stood up and walked his bicycle out of the restaurant. Collin stayed seated and followed Willie with his eyes as he disappeared from sight. Collin remained unmoving and still saturated in something unspeakable.

"Would you like another refill on your coffee?" said a server who knelt down beside him.

Collin looked into her eyes, as if for the first time, and felt as though he'd know her his whole life. This moment seemed so new yet so familiar that Collin Hartley could not discern between the two.

"No, thank you," he said, "I'm actually leaving soon."

The server looked compassionately at Collin and asked, "Are you all right, sir?"

"Yes," Collin replied. "Yes, I'm fine."

Then Collin stood up while the server watched him cautiously. It seemed to her that Collin could faint and fall over at any time. She held her hands out in case he fell and watched as he tossed his money near his empty coffee cup. Then the server followed Collin Hartley with her eyes as he vanished through the front door of Renee's.

Collin stood on the sidewalk outside Renee's and debated over how he'd get to work. What's interesting is that this internal debate did not occur solely with his mind. He could feel this debate through the entirety of himself. It even seemed intuitive since it was not centered in any one specific part of the whole. He could feel his options in his very blood. One half of Collin pleaded a case for walking to work down Sheffield Avenue and the other half for running down the train tracks. And before this debate really got started, Collin felt the stronger impulse to walk come over him.

So, Collin Hartley walked south on Sheffield Avenue, enthralled with his place in the tapestry of organic life that he observed. The disappearance of the cars and public transportation made everything quiet; in fact, this scene even appeared soft and supple. Instead of the screeching tires and obnoxious horns, there was the pitter patter of feet and the humming along to familiar songs. The lines of direction drawn by all of the people surrounding him were like the branches of a tree. He saw people coming together at intersections like a tree trunk and then they veered apart and vanished into thin air. As Collin walked, he witnessed everything in perpetual motion. Nothing remained still. All the various fragments moved about like living patterns and almost dancing to a nearly inaudible music. And Collin Hartley added his own lines and pattern to this tapestry of organic life.

He took Sheffield south to Chicago Avenue and then zigzagged over to Restful Eternities. He stood in front of the sign again and looked up at the moon. It seemed that he welcomed it to come forth like the day before, but the moon was small and it stayed imprisoned within the confines of its borders. After a few more moments, Collin walked through the entrance and up to the second floor.

When Collin entered the calling area, he knew that things had returned to normal. He heard the phones ringing and he listened to his coworkers pleading their sales pitches. Collin looked at the dry erase board and saw Tim writing in new monthly selling goals. Tim looked over at Collin, then at his wristwatch and then back at Collin again.

Tim shook his head saying, "At this point I don't think it really matters if you're late, Collin. So just go do whatever you like. Go buy another bed… go talk to our buyers about the meaning of life and death… I just don't care any more…"

Collin didn't say a word to Tim, nor did he exhibit a single gesture or facial expression. Instead, Collin walked towards his cubicle as a creature unto himself. As he neared his cube, Allen approached him with enthusiastic eyes and an uplifted spirit.

"Collin Hartley," Allen said, "I talked to Mel Leimer last night and I scheduled an appointment to visit the school tomorrow morning."

Collin smiled and replied, "That's good… I hope you find what you're looking for there, Allen."

Collin entered his cubicle and tossed his coat in the corner; Allen followed him close behind and this nearness made Collin uncomfortable. Collin even felt irritated and trapped by Allen. But Collin remembered 'Be As It May' and also to not display his negative emotions, so he did not project this irritability out towards Allen. Collin saw this happening as an event that had fallen to his lot, and he was determined to treat Allen as cheerfully and honestly as he could. So all of this helped Collin to get over himself and to live in the moment as a human being.

"Your excitement is contagious, Allen," said Collin. "Truly, I wish for your happiness."

Then Allen extended his hand to Collin and said, "Really, Collin, thank you for telling me about this school. I feel like you've opened up a new opportunity for me."

They shook hands and Collin replied, "I'm happy for you, Allen. Just remember to ask yourself if this is the type of instruction you really want while you're observing there tomorrow."

"I've been asking myself all kinds of questions since yesterday," responded Allen. "I've been questioning this school... this job... and really just questioning what I want from my life..."

Collin nodded his head sympathetically and Allen continued, "So, as it stands right now... I'm going to check out this painting school tomorrow and see what I think. And as far as the job is concerned, I've decided to start working with my cousin the Monday after next."

"So, you've decided to go work with your cousin," remarked Collin.

"Yes," said Allen, "I've decided to make some changes in my life and work is just one of them. And I know that working with my cousin will be essentially the same as working here, but it will give a little more freedom. You know… it'll be easier for me to take time off… to invest my time in other things…"

"That's excellent," Collin replied. "I wish you the best in this new life you're creating for yourself."

Allen just smiled, as he walked backwards out of Collin's cubicle, and said, "I'll let you know on Monday how everything goes this weekend. I'm really looking forward to seeing the school and meeting Mel and Nancy."

Collin grinned as Allen left his cube and then he turned towards his calling list to prepare himself for the day. He looked over the names and numbers and he questioned how he could struggle with himself in this process. At first, he thought about maybe changing the order in which he called people, just like he did the day before, but then he decided against it. Then he thought about changing his sales pitch, but this wasn't agreeable either. Collin even considered standing on one leg while he made his calls, but this obviously wouldn't float with Tim at the office.

After some careful considering, Collin decided to sit in a different way. He chose to position himself on the ground with the backs of his feet flat to the floor and with his rump resting on his heels. This position was extremely uncomfortable for Collin, so he decided that he would only keep this posture for a few minutes at a time.

Collin began his calls while rotating between this new sitting position and then replacing it with others that were more bearable. He would make one call in this new position and then the next would be with one that was more comfortable for him. Call after call and one posture after another, Collin made his notorious sales pitch. And like most days, Collin worked the entire morning without closing a single deal.

When the early afternoon came around, Collin took a break and enjoyed a few moments of silence for himself. This was the time that he'd normally break for lunch but since that was no longer an option, he decided to feed himself with quiet. Allen even offered to treat Collin to Subway, but he regretfully declined. Collin Hartley just sat in silence as the whole calling floor cleared and his coworkers disappeared into The Land of Lunch. It was only after everyone had left, that Collin's phone rang.

Before answering it, Collin considered for a moment who it might be. And in the same way he debated with himself in front of Renee's, this considering happened through the whole of himself and it was not centered solely in his mind. This considering wasn't specific to any one specific part of Collin Hartley, so it seemed like a balanced considering of his whole being.

So, Collin's being first considered that maybe this call was Danny Alvero from Somber Incorporated following up on the sale of the Levibed Adventurer. Then Collin considered that maybe it was his brother or maybe even the Mysterious William Green. After this short series of considering, Collin answered the phone and eagerly awaited the identity of the caller to be revealed.

"Is this Collin Hartley?" asked the caller.

"Yes," Collin replied, "this is Collin Hartley from Restful Eternities."

"Hey, Collin, this is John."

"John," inquired Collin.

"Yes," said John. "We talked on the phone earlier this week. We talked about death and then I bought a grave plot from you."

"Oh yes, John," replied Collin. "How are you?"

"Well, I've been thinking a lot about our talk. I've been thinking over the life/death question, and I've come to the conclusion that you're right. Our call had an impact on me."

"What do you mean?" Collin asked.

John remained silent for a moment and then responded, "I mean there really is no solution to the life/death question. Nothing totally satisfying. The life/death question is our ignorance of what is beyond this life. We just don't know. But Seeking truth is our awakening. Or to put it another way, I think the life/death question is our sleep and our quest for Truth is our awakening."

"So, where are you in relation to all of this?" asked Collin.

"Oh, I'm clearly asleep," said John. "I'm totally engrossed in the life/death question. All I've been thinking about is why do we live and why do we die? But I've been feeling like I want to get away from all of this. I feel in my heart that I want something more substantial… something closer to truth."

Then Collin explained, "It was related to me one time that it's important for us to first realize our ignorance before we can realize our truth. It's like saying that we must first experience our sleep before we can experience waking up from sleep. In a way the sleep is part of the awakening."

"See, that's why I'm calling you," said John. "I don't know how you wake up. What does that mean? And I don't know what it means to realize our ignorance or to realize our truth. These are all just words to me. But I feel like I want to know the truth… the desire to awaken is somehow in me… but I don't know how to begin…"

"It is the only thing that happens," replied Collin. "Really. Everything is just waking up. Rocks waken to tress, waken to worms, waken to bees, waken to monkeys, waken to human beings… then we awaken to Divinity."

Then John became most sincere and asked, "So where do I go from here? I'm confused? My mind is my biggest enemy."

Collin responded, "Calm the mind. Find a way to calm the mind. Maybe meditation. Music. Painting. Focus on sacred images. Repeat the Names of God."

"Yes, calm the mind," said John. "I need to calm the mind."

"Maybe a good starting point," replied Collin, "your wish to experience the awakening and calming the mind. The second point is to remain totally present focused. Be here now. Third, you should be honest with yourself. And do the best you can to love God wholeheartedly."

Then John asked, "How can I love God wholeheartedly if God is unseen? How can I truly love God if I don't see or understand the Infinite One? Again, these are all just words."

Collin answered, "I believe that's why you begin with the wish to love God wholeheartedly. As it stands now this is an aim… to try love God even though God cannot be seen or understood. This is all part of developing a relationship with God."

Collin paused for a moment to reposition the way he was sitting and then continued, "Are you familiar with the messages given by Meher Baba of India?"

John told him no and Collin explained, "Well, Meher Baba was a God-Man who was in our midst during the first half of the twentieth century. Among many messages that he communicated to humanity, the most important was the need for people to love God. He told his followers that the aim of life is to love God completely and that the goal of life is to become One with God. He also discussed the nature of taking steps towards God and the efforts that were needed to attain this highest goal. Meher Baba also said that the spiritual suffering that occurs while taking these steps towards God are the most acute, but he also said that reaching the goal was worth all of the physical and mental suffering in the whole universe."

"Are you a follower of this Meher Baba?" asked John.

Collin replied, "I love Meher Baba and I am totally inspired by His life and messages. I pay special attention to the messages of all God realized Souls. So yes, I would say I follow Baba. But I take steps towards The Divine in my own way. I have mostly been inclined toward the Impersonal Aspect of God. As the Infinite and Eternal One. In the abstract. The Spirit that moves in all things."

"Tell me more about the Impersonal aspect of God," asked John.

"I should only leave you with the name itself," said Collin. "Important that you have your own path to God. One that makes sense to you."

"And what if I want you to help guide me?" asked John.

"Then call me back," replied Collin, "and I will be available to you. Still, you should think over a path that makes sense to you."

The two of them sat in silence for many minutes. This period of silence would have been uncomfortable if it happened during a normal conversation. But these two men were not having a normal conversation. They were sharing ideas and pieces of their self that neither shared with just anyone. So this silence was natural and it gave them the proper time to digest certain information.

"What kinds of changes have you noticed while taking steps towards God?" asked John.

Collin replied, "At times there is a sense of detachment from the worldly, but this detachment is very difficult to describe. For instance, there are times when I feel detached when I am talking to people, but it's a detachment of the inner observer. I still experience all the thoughts, sensations and emotions that go with it, but there is a deeper part that is relatively free from it. So to detach doesn't necessarily mean having a cold attitude towards the thing you're detached from. To be detached means that it doesn't have an effect on the deeper parts of Self. So you see… this is all difficult to describe. To be detached in a conversation means that you're talking but you're not talking. You converse but you're not attached to the conversation itself."

Then Collin became more thoughtful and said, "I like the abstract. I like aesthetic. I only have moments of this type of detachment… only short intervals of time when I experience this relative inner freedom. The majority of my time is spent making efforts to control the senses so that this inner freedom is created. I work to still the mind and to walk in the direction of God."

"In what direction is God?" asked John.

Collin said, "How can there be a direction to God if God is Omnipresent? God is in everything, but we have to develop the eyes to see Him. Until then, God remains unseen and unfathomable. However, we have been given all the Ways to see God, but we have to apply these Ways. Like opening the eyes. That is why we begin with the wish to love God and the wish to become One with Him."

"That is my understanding at his point of awakening."

"This rattles the brain doesn't it, Collin?" said John.

Collin paused for a moment to sense his body in its new sitting position. He felt uncomfortable but it helped him to experience his Being.

Then Collin said, "My opinion, is that our mind can disrupt our Being and this conversation is a perfect example. Here we are, two lost sheep, talking about finding the Good Shepherd. All the while He is present. Maybe more about seeing than understanding and thinking."

"Do you believe that God helps us while we search for Him?" asked John.

"My opinion is that God is the Creator and the Creation, God is The Destination and The Way," replied Collin. "I would say that God's love and mercy make the impossible something possible."

Then Collin became more thoughtful and continued, "A dear friend of mine once told me that God matches you step for step along The Way. He says that each step towards God is a step that God takes towards you."

"I wonder if prayer is a real step towards God," remarked John.

"I've thought a lot about that myself over the years," said Collin.

"Any conclusions?" asked John.

Collin responded, "Well, it seems to me that it depends on the type of prayer and the intention behind it. For example, it only stands to reason that a prayer done out of love for God is of a higher order than a prayer done for material gain. The prayer done for love of God is a devotional type whereas the prayer for material gain is of a low type. I sometimes use 'The Lord's Prayer' and instead of reciting it dryly through the mind I work to bring this prayer into the heart. This is one way to step towards God and to commune with The Divine. Bring it into the heart."

"That's interesting," said John. "I've never really considered praying from the heart. Of course, I haven't been consistent with prayer anyway since I was a boy. But even then, all I remember is the dry repetition of

'The Lord's Prayer' in my mind. I never felt it in my heart."

Collin said, "That's why we have to start with the wish to love God. If we were honest with ourselves, we would admit that it can seem impossible to love God. If you have true love for God then you probably don't need to pray. But for most of us, we have to begin with the wish to bring God into our heart."

"What's it like," asked John, "being in love with God wholeheartedly? Is this the ecstatic states that the saints experienced?"

"I don't know," replied Collin. "I try to be an aspirant myself. I'm still making efforts to love God wholeheartedly. I have glimpses of this love but then those moments disappear. When I think about Saints, I do believe it's possible that their ecstatic states were a result of Divine Love. As I believe St. Francis of Assisi merged with God and was intoxicated in His Divine Love. The stigmata, his love of people and suffering for the sake of others were all examples of this Divine Love."

At that moment, Collin Hartley repositioned himself again on the floor. This time he laid down flat on his back with his head towards the telephone. He aligned himself symmetrically and then waited for John to speak.

"It's funny," said John, "I actually went to church this past week and the priest discoursed on the same principles you are talking about. He discussed the pillars of Jesus Christ's teachings. He spoke about loving God with all of your mind, all of your heart and all of yourself. And also loving your neighbor as you love yourself."

"I don't think that we discussed that," said Collin. "Having a wish to love our neighbor…"

Then John chuckled and said, "And that's just it! I don't know if I really know how to love at all! And here I am talking about loving God and my neighbor! I'm a fool."

Collin replied sincerely, "Maybe a fool. Maybe honest. Maybe both. I think you see more about your position than you think. You see the condition of your heart and without seeing this, you wouldn't be able to open it. So keep seeing and keep opening up."

"And this brings us back to the subject of Ways," said John. "I need the support of other people for this seeing to happen. I need a community of people that I can awaken with and develop Being with. And I'm going to take your advice, Collin. I'm going to research Ways… but in the meantime, I think I'll start attending church regularly and try praying from my heart."

Collin replied, "Yes, John, and remember that you've already begun awakening. There is only awakening. Just on a continuum. Your wish to love God, your wish to be honest with yourself and your very wish to awaken is your beginning. And when you choose A Way out of the wilderness, remember to endure patiently through the rough terrain with love, hope and faith in The Unseen."

"Thank you, Collin," said John. "Thank you for sharing all of this with me."

"Call me anytime," replied Collin Hartley, "since I'm sure you have my number."

John laughed and replied jokingly, "Yes, as it turns out, my investment in Restful Eternities has many perks. I mean, I'm getting this free spiritual counseling for my investment in death."

"Well, take advantage," said Collin, "I'm only here for a few more weeks."

Then John responded, "Maybe we'll be able to meet in person then. I'd like to see you face to face, Collin."

"Yes," said Collin, "this would be something to look forward to. Friendship developed in the pursuit of The Infinite Ocean of Love is the highest!"

Then the two became silent. It was the quiet recognition that their time together was almost over. Then Collin shared his parting words.

"Well, peace be with you, Brother John."

John replied, "And peace be with you, Collin Hartley."

Then Collin hung up the phone and closed his eyes to the glare of the fluorescent lights above him.

Chapter Six: The Shoes

Collin Hartley woke up. Although he didn't really wake up since he only slept a few hours during the night. So it was more like Collin Hartley opened his eyes. He turned his head to look out the bedroom window and it was then the tears began streaming down the sides of his face. Collin's whole body ached, and his fear and desperation only added to this suffering. He felt helpless and alone that morning, and the only relief he felt was in knowing that it was Saturday. So, Collin wiped away the tears and he sighed as a recognition of the weekend. Then he sat up and rubbed his face in the wilderness of sheets and pillows. Tarazina sprinted across the bedroom floor and then sprung into Collin's lap. She looked up at him almost smiling, so it was no wonder that Collin's mood began to change.

He petted the cat and said, "I love you, girl. I love you too…"

Then he scratched the top of her head and continued, "How can I become as hopeful and faithful as you? Just look at you… a beautiful creature that doesn't ask any questions. You live in the moment with complete faith and you love indiscriminately."

The lovely Tarazina just purred and purred while Collin scratched her head. The sunlight flickered in her yellow eyes and the corners of her mouth turned upwards in ecstasy.

"Really," said Collin, "I wonder if life is really the same for all sentient beings? I know that we think it's different… but what if life, in even the seemingly darkest places, is really beautiful? Maybe we just miss the beauty by the way we interpret the pain?"

Then Tarazina started licking Collin's hand and this made him smile. The sensation tickled his hand and warmed his chest, and all of this uplifted his spirit.

"Well, girl," he said enthusiastically, "I think I'm about ready to crawl out of my dark corner and journey outside."

Then he stood up and folded his sheets where afterwards he cut a path to the back porch to freshen up. He skipped the bathroom since he knew it was useless at this point and he grabbed a kitchen towel while he walked past his empty cupboards and desolate pantry. When Collin opened the back door and stepped out onto the porch, he could see a thaw happening. Water dripped from the rooftops and only puddles remained of the former ice and snow. It seemed to him that there was even the faint smell of spring in the air. Things appeared cleaner and fresher.

So Collin stood near the edge of the porch where water was falling all over. It seemed like a regular shower to Collin since the water was still cold. He rubbed the water onto all the necessary parts and then patted himself dry with the kitchen towel.

Afterwards, Collin did visit the bathroom, but it was only to comb his hair and to put deodorant on his underarms. He noticed then, as he did the day before, that even though his body ached as though it were dying, he still appeared to look healthier. Collin looked in the mirror while he combed his hair and he seemed vibrant and alive. This was strange for him since he felt that he was more like a walking corpse. However, Collin took this observation for what it was and then went into the east room of his apartment to complete his morning exercise. How you feel and how you look do not always align.

Collin assumed his position on the floor and began the exercise by relaxing the whole. He aligned himself vertically and then he fine-tuned this posture into complete symmetry. Collin also attended to his breathing rhythm without altering it in any way. Then Collin closed his eyes and moved about the whole. The two days of fasting made him hollow and at times his mind couldn't help but liken this experience to that of a reed flute. So Collin directed his consciousness throughout the whole, all the while a tune was being played through him. And since it was the weekend, Collin added a series of prayers onto the exercise. So on the inhale Collin repeated, "Lord Jesus Christ Son of God," and then on the exhale, "have mercy upon me a sinner." Over and over again he repeated this prayer and all the while working to bring this mantra into his heart. Then after the repetition of the Jesus Prayer, Collin recited 'The Lord's Prayer'. This one also resonated from his heart and these prayers taken together were in fact Collin's true longing for communion with The Unseen Source.

After the meditation exercise, Collin went into the bedroom to get dressed, and when he opened the closet, he discovered the new vanishing of the day. All of his shoes, in fact all of his footwear, was missing. The shoes, the boots and the sandals were all gone. Collin just grinned as he was not really fazed by this new disappearance. Then he opened his dresser drawer and saw that even his socks were gone. However, this didn't have much of an effect on Collin either. He just went about dressing the rest of himself with complete faith in this new perception.

Collin looked down at his bare feet and said jokingly, "Well, you're exposed now. It'll be just me and you on this walk. And I got a feeling that it might be rough. So be careful and keep your toes peeled."

His toes just wiggled up at him as if saying, "All right, Chief!"

Collin opened up the front door to his apartment and there stood the cardboard box like a great monolith. The face of the box had the massive words: The Levibed Adventurer written across the center, and in the corner was the name and address of Somber Incorporated. Collin stood near the shadows edge and looked at it for a few moments. He wondered if there was in fact merchandise in the box or if it was empty. Again, Collin waited just a few seconds before reaching out to touch this enigma. Then finally, he stretched out his arms and wrapped his fingers around the far corners of the box. Collin Hartley lifted the monolith and discovered that it was empty. He brought the box into his living room and leaned it up against the wall. He didn't bother opening it since he thought that he might investigate the insides later. He was sure that there was no bed in the box, but he thought that there might be other useful information. After he rested the box securely against the wall, he left the apartment and headed down the stairs; on the way he bumped into Ms Weeks in the hallway as she was leaving her apartment too.

"Someone has a big delivery today," she said to Collin Hartley.

"Yes," he replied, "that is my new Levibed Adventurer."

"A Levibed Adventurer," she inquired. "What is that, Mr Collin?"

"Well, Ms Weeks," he said, "the Levibed Adventurer is a bed that's going to revolutionize the world of sleep. It's a bed that levitates you in the air at night when you slumber."

Ms Weeks howled and replied, "Oh, Mr Collin! How is this possible?"

Collin chuckled and said, "Well, this bed levitates you through the emission of electromagnetic currents and from what I hear it gives you a more restful night's sleep than an average box spring and mattress."

Ms Weeks shook her head in disbelief and said, "My, my… this technology is even creeping into our bedrooms. Eeehh… what will they come up with next?"

It was then that Collin looked down and saw Ms Weeks' feet. They were the feet of a woman who'd been cramming them into shoes a few sizes too small all of her life. Her toes were gnarled and they overlapped each other like lattice work. This disfiguring was a sign of suffering and Collin couldn't help but associate her feet with the fakirs he had heard about in India. The fakirs are people who put their bodies into impossible postures for years at a time and some, it seemed, were able to turn their bodies into pretzels. The results of which were often the complete disfiguring of the body. And these fakirs practice this 'art' as a way to get beyond the body; their practices are intended for taking steps towards God. So as Collin looked on at Ms Weeks' feet and associated them to the fakirs in India, he couldn't help but pay homage to them (even though her disfiguring was the apparent result of vanity rather than the true longing for God).

Then Collin Hartley turned his attention towards his own feet. In comparison to Ms Weeks, his feet were well pedicured; they were smooth and even effeminate. Collin's impression of his own feet was that they had never really known real work and suffering. They were like his soft and well-manicured hands. Collin's feet and hands only knew of subtle work. His hands prepared tea and they operated the phone at work, and his feet were cushioned by sensible shoes that absorbed the burdens of all his walking. However, Collin knew that this was all about to change since he was entering into the world barefoot.

"So are we still on for dinner this Friday?" Ms Weeks asked.

"Of course," Collin replied. "How could I ever pass on your company, Ms Weeks?"

Then she rubbed Collin's right arm and said excitedly, "And my niece is looking forward to meeting you, Mr Collin! She is really an angel sent from Heaven!"

"That will be nice," he said, "and I'm sure we'll all have a good time."

Then the two walked out of the building. They stood together outside and breathed in the fresh air around them.

"This feels more like April than January," Ms Weeks remarked.

"Yes," replied Collin, "it's really beautiful today."

Afterwards, Ms Weeks said goodbye and Collin remained standing at the front of the building as she disappeared from his sight. Collin continued to absorb the impressions that surrounded him while he exchanged air with The Creation. He saw people running around everywhere and the pitter patter of their feet was the melody that their hearts sang to. People were still racing up and down the streets while pretending to drive cars, only now they were barefoot and this made sounds like clapping. In fact, it seemed to Collin that there were layers to this clapping music. Some of the people clapped quietly while they walked on sidewalks, others clapped more boldly as they jogged past those walking, and still others clapped thunderously while they raced around in the streets; each one of them was a different size, weight and measure. And this created different tempos, different rhythms and a series of different beats, but somehow it all worked together as One musical piece. This was a feet-clapping symphony with many variations of tone, pitch and tambour.

Then Collin began walking himself and added his own ingredient to this orchestra. He sort of shuffled his feet and made a brushing sound while he walked. It was a shhh, shhh type of sound. Then he closed his eyes to feel the brushing of his feet against the sidewalk. He felt the shhh, shhh softly reverberate up through his legs. Then he paused and then stepped again. Collin did this for a mile or so, sometimes focusing on his own shhh, shhh and other times listening to how his sound mixed with all of the other sounds. Sometimes he closed his eyes and other times they were open. Collin constantly appreciated the diversity in this feet-clapping symphony as he walked along. He heard the deep and slow flwaps of big, fat feet and he heard the mouse-like scants of scrambling little feet. And there again was his own shhh, shhh sound. All the while this harmony uplifted Collin and played into him like music for his soul.

Then Collin began walking as he usually did with no shuffling or brushing of the feet. He walked with one foot in front of the other and he sensed his connection with the ground beneath. He sensed the cool concrete of the sidewalk and his nerve endings registering the texture with each step. Then Collin stepped off of the sidewalk and wandered through someone's front yard. The ground was moist and the grass cleaned his feet while he walked through it. And then Collin stopped, he stood in the middle of the yard and sensed his connection with the earth. He noticed an intimacy between his bare feet and the naked earth. It reminded him of something the Mysterious William Green had said to him earlier in the week. Collin felt his flesh against the earth's flesh and he sensed the verticality of his long body protruding upwards like an antenna. Then he closed his eyes and envisioned all the people of the earth also like antennae. He saw billions of people resonating frequencies through their bodies, all of them transmitting The Song of God to the earth.

Then Collin opened his eyes and staggered a few paces away from the center of the yard. He experienced what seemed like contractions, so he became disoriented and hunched over. It had been more than two days since Collin had consumed food or drink and it was again having an effect on his body. He sensed his physical self being wrung out like a wet dish towel. And with this wringing out came the desires, opinions and tendencies of the flesh. So, Collin's body was dying and he knew this while he worked to balance himself. He even thought he might fall to the ground and lick the moisture from the grass. However, Collin did not; instead, he walked back to the sidewalk and pushed onward with his journey.

The familiar duality of really dying and really coming to life was realized while he walked. Collin's flesh was withering but something inside was also waking up. So there was the experience of extreme suffering and also joyous rapture at the same time. What Collin found most amazing was that this inner joyous celebration could not be shown outside of him. There was simply no way to express it. He even caught a reflection of himself in a store window and thought, "This external mirage does not show what's really going on inside of me." Then he stepped closer to observe the very neutral expression on his face. He was going to try smiling but at that moment he knew it was insincere, so he didn't.

After this observation, Collin walked a few miles west to Margate Park. He hoped to see Willie there, but he didn't really have any expectations. As he walked around the park, it seemed to him that feet everywhere were carrying on conversations. The children's feet talked to mommy's feet, husband's feet talked to their wife's feet and friends' feet talked to friends' feet all over. And Collin couldn't help but eavesdrop in on some of these conversations.

He saw some little kids' feet running around their mother's feet asking, "Can we go to the beach and walk in the sand? Please, Mommy, please…"

Then the mother's feet responded, "No, my little darlings… it's January. I know that it's nice today but we're not going to the beach."

So the toes of the little kids pouted as their feet stopped dead in their tracks.

Then the mother's feet said sternly, "Okay… if you're going to be like that then I guess we'll just go back home! And you can all play in your bedrooms today!"

The children's toes popped up and their feet pleaded, "No, Mommy, no! We want to be outside today! Besides… the kitty cat peed in our bedroom this morning! Please don't make us play on the wet carpet! Stinks in there! Please, Mommy, please let us stay outside!"

Then the mother's feet said factually, "Well, who wanted the cat in the first place? Was it me? Was it your dad?"

The toes of the little kids pouted again and they replied, "We love our kitty cat. She can't help that she pees on the carpet. She gets nervous… that's all…"

"Okay, enough cat talk," the mother's feet said sharply.

Collin's own feet seemed to smile as they turned from the conversation between the mom and her children; his feet looked to the right and they began perceiving something new. The feet of two lovers walked by in the shadow of a maple tree. His feet were muscular, and her feet were dainty and beautifully groomed.

His feet said, "I love taking walks with you on the weekend. It feels like it's just us. The work week is done and we finally get to enjoy one another."

Then they stopped and she rubbed her soft toes over the sides of his feet saying, "Yes, we get to enjoy each other all day long."

At that moment, Collin noticed that his feet were staring so he turned them yet again in the direction of another conversation. His feet saw the feet of two homeless men as they dangled from a nearby tree stump. These feet seemed somewhat chummy and like they were friends.

"Do you smell that?" asked the one pair of feet.

"Smell what?" the other responded defensively.

"That's the smell of spring in the air," said the former.

"You're crazy," replied the defensive feet. "Spring is still a few months away."

"Yeah, I know… but it still doesn't hurt to sneak a peek at our friend, spring. You know that spring is for the homeless man."

Then the other feet said, "Well, today is our day then... I guess..."

"Yes," said the former, "what do you say we go down to the beach and cover ourselves with sand?"

"That's fine by me," said the friend, "that's fine by me."

Collin Hartley walked past all of these talking feet and then strolled through the grass at Margate Park. The feeling of spring was certainly in the air, but the ground was still cold even though the snow had melted. The soil squished some, but it was still frozen solid at the same time. Collin's feet convulsed at times due to this cold. They even seemed to shiver and wrap invisible arms around themselves to keep warm. Then Collin stopped in the middle of the park and looked down at these little creatures. They seemed like they were his own, yet not his own at the same time; it was much like the world around him which also seemed his own yet not his own.

Then Collin kneeled down and pressed his ear to the ground. The wet grass made his ear moist and somehow scratchy. Then he pushed it further into the soil. A suction happened between the ear and the ground. It was then that he heard the bowels of the earth churning and grumbling. Collin was listening in on some of her internal processes. It reminded him of putting an ear to another person's stomach where the digestion of substances could be heard. Then he thought that maybe it was his own stomach he was listening to.

He thought that maybe this suction only helped him to hear his own internal processes rather than the earth's.

After this listening, Collin lifted his head and then investigated the ground with his hands. He combed his fingers through the grass and rubbed his palms over the belly of the earth. It was a massaging action and this even appeared to warm up that part of the ground. Then Collin brought his eyes near to his hands and looked while his fingers brushed through the blades of green grass. He saw a gallery of color in that micro-forest. He saw the greens, browns, blacks and greys. And he also saw tiny prisms of color in the beaded water. He observed the hues of indigo, yellow and red that he'd never seen before. These colors were resilient and electric in character.

It was then that Collin heard the laughing. He raised his head up and saw a group of homeless guys pointing their fingers at him. They sipped their pretend beers and fell over each other in hysteria. Then a few even asked Collin to please continue groping the dirt. They told him that they were sorry for the interruption and requested that he go on. And to all of this Collin said nothing; instead, he came to his feet and walked away.

After leaving the park, Collin Hartley decided to visit a church in Andersonville. It was a Catholic church and it was his favorite in the whole city of Chicago. Collin loved this church owing more to the way it felt rather than the way it looked. There are certainly more beautiful churches by appearance, but this one had a beauty in 'presence'. There was something about its posture and its poise that made it so lovely. Sure, it had the beautiful stained glass, byzantine arches and gorgeous stonework found in many traditional churches. However, Collin suspected that maybe it was the people that attended the church that made it so breath taking. He believed that it was the people that gave the church this unique presence and not in an allegorical way.

Collin approached the church just as the afternoon services were letting out. He saw the brothers, sisters, mothers and fathers walk out of the front doors. Their feet were clean and their selves refreshed as they flooded the streets. Collin walked past the people and towards the back parking lot of the church so he could meditate on the stained-glass cross in the rear. There was something spectacular in seeing this cross in the afternoon light of the sun. At times it was as if Heaven opened a porthole to the earth through this stained-glass cross.

So Collin Hartley stood at the center of the empty parking lot and meditated on the cross. He knew that the cross symbolized the crucifixion of Jesus Christ, but he also understood intuitively that it communicated something mysterious also. And it was the mystery of this something else that Collin attended to. He meditated deeply while reciting the Jesus Prayer, the whole time working to bring this prayer into his heart. He inhaled, "Lord Jesus Christ Son of God," and then exhaled, "have mercy upon me a sinner." Over and over again, Collin observed his own longing to perceive Total Truth and Divinity.

Then a door opened to the side of the cross and out walked the head priest of the church. He walked towards Collin while occasionally glancing back at the stained-glass cross. He was an elderly man with kind eyes. He was portly and he had a friendly disposition.

"Good morning to you," he said to Collin.

"Good morning, Father," Colin replied while keeping half of his attention of the cross.

"Oh no, my brother," said the priest. "We have but one Father and he's in Heaven. Please… just call me Thomas."

Collin smiled and said, "Good morning, Brother Thomas… I'm Collin Hartley."

"I don't recall having met you before, Brother Collin," said Thomas. "Is this your first time at our church?"

"No, Thomas," Collin replied, "I come here once a week to meditate on the cross. I was raised Catholic and I feel a love for the life of Jesus. I practice some of the prayers and practices of the faith. Currently I have embraced the influence of Avatar Meher Baba."

Then Thomas looked at the stained glass cross and remarked, "Do you know that St. Francis of Assisi was enthralled with the cross?"

Thomas returned his eyes to Collin and continued, "He meditated on it constantly… the cross is a very powerful symbol and very few have been able to tap into its true inner meaning. Many are drawn to it but most only see the cross as the instrument of Jesus' death."

Collin said, "It's interesting this play between the inner and outer. On the surface there is the crucifixion but within there is something mysterious."

Thomas smiled slyly and responded, "Yes, Brother Collin, the cross does have both inner and outer qualities. There is an inner and outer content just as there is with the church itself."

"What do you mean, Brother Thomas?" Collin asked.

Then Thomas explained, "The Church accommodates the whole variation of followers, so we have content for those more drawn to the worldly and then there is content for those with an affinity for the inner life. Some are more akin to the outer forms of worship while others long for deeper truth. So as a priest I develop services for these different types. For those committed to the outer forms of worship, we have weekly Mass, special holiday services and we also give them access to the church itself twenty-four hours each day. All of this to support them in their outer worship. And for those drawn towards deeper truth we have confessionals, small work groups and special Sunday gatherings. These confessionals and small work groups are meant to support individuals in their own work of Self-Realization."

Collin asked, "What kinds of exercises do you use in these small work groups? Are they exercises that keep with the inner tradition or have you tried something new?"

Thomas said, "We do keep with the inner Christian tradition but the specific exercises we use depend on the members of each group; we have a few different groups. Some groups focus on daily prayers and meditations while others work more intensely on Self-Realization. However, the groups that labor for Self-Realization are very small in number. In fact, out of the thousands that make up our congregation only a handful participate in these Self-Realization groups."

"Do you mind me asking what kinds of work you do in these groups, Brother Thomas?"

Thomas looked at Collin compassionately and explained, "Really, I can tell you very little about these groups since the very foundation of them is extremely personal. You see, the specific work we do in these groups has to remain between the aspirant, the group itself and The Lord Our Father. Nothing can be shared outside of the group. It is an inner tradition and one step on a very intimate path being tread by the Lover. However, it will do no harm to share a few basic pieces of information with you.

First of all, a person has to get qualified to enter into a group. Each individual must begin in a group that works with prayer and meditation. Once they've developed far enough in the prayer and meditation groups then they get qualified to enter into an advanced Self-Realization group. But entering this group is no easy thing. Once an aspirant enters the group, their dedication to practices is increased tenfold. And because the work in these groups is so strenuous, we have to support each other through various means. All those who participate in the Self-Realization groups must live in strict accordance with the wishes laid down by Jesus Christ. So, we have various practices that help the aspirant to live the wish of God and none of this is easy. We meet often to support each other, discuss our falls and shortcomings. We encourage and inspire to help each other to rise again and move on."

"Do you observe fasts and other renunciations?" Collin asked.

"We observe many types of renunciations," said Thomas, "but please understand that I cannot share any details with you, Brother Collin. Our sacrifices and renunciations have to remain between us and The Lord Our God."

It was then that the two took a moment of silence and gazed upon the cross. The image was illuminated and it bathed these brothers in light.

Then Thomas broke this silence and said, "If you're interested in all that we've discussed, Brother Collin, please join us for services this Thursday. The church welcomes you and we invite you into our community of worship. Afterwards, you can meet with myself and Brother Robert and we can talk more about the inner traditions we have here at our church. If that seems a path you would like to pursue."

Collin Hartley told Thomas that he would consider the invitation and then the two of them parted. Brother Thomas ventured out into the neighborhood and Brother Collin went south in the direction of his apartment. As Collin walked, he could feel the return of the aching in his body and the withering of his flesh. Then he experienced another set of contractions and with it the terror of his body dying. However, the inner man was still very much alive, and it pushed the outer carcass along effortlessly like a feather.

Collin decided to stop at the park on Leland and Ashland to observe the families that congregated there. He sat on a patch of grass where a bench was once erected and looked out at all the playfulness around him. He saw some young boys tossing around a football and playing their own variation of the sport. There wasn't an inkling of competition between them and it really seemed more like hot potato than anything else. These boys, like all the others at the park, were truly enjoying each other's company.

Then Collin saw mothers and fathers wrestling with their babies in the grass, he saw lovers holding one another in the shadows of trees and he saw friends sharing the intimate stories of their lives. And Collin Hartley lived vicariously through all of these people as he associated their experiences with his own. He remembered wrestling with his own niece and nephew, tossing the pigskin around with his brother and cousins and he remembered sharing intimate moments with previous girlfriends. Collin felt his love of consciousness at that moment; it was the essence of all other loves, and it was but another familiar glimpse of something pure and simple. Then that glimpse vanished as his body screamed again in terror.

The cold sweat gushed from his pores, his hands turned cold and clammy, and he felt tears well up in his eyes. But then the body relaxed as it was reminded that it could not afford the loss of moisture. So the tears sank back into his eyes and the sweat soaked back into his skin.

It was then that Collin saw the most beautiful feet in the world come near him. Their tone was brown, their shape supple and the toes diminished perfectly in size from the big toe to the pinky. These feet expressed an angelic nature, they were sensitive, compassionate yet strong at the same time. These feet approached him gracefully and were almost feline in their movements.

Then he heard from above, "My beloved, your pain and your pleasure are equal in the eye of The Divine. They are both there to show the intensity of your living. The intensity of life force. The intensity of your love."

When Collin looked up, he was certain that he was in the presence of an angel sent from Heaven. Her long black hair fell voluptuously over her shoulders. Her face and her eyes were illuminated like the stained-glass crucifix at Brother Thomas' church. She wore a white summer dress that complimented her bronze skin and her quiet hands slept at her sides as if tucked away in dreams at night.

She said, "Have faith in what is being born, my beloved, the birthing pains will soon be replaced with a joy that no mind has ever conceived."

Then she knelt down and her hands awakened as they moved up and sat upon her thighs. She smiled at Collin Hartley and then continued.

"The pains of dying and the pains of being born overlap each other, but these pains will bring a Life Everlasting. These pains are of the Mother giving birth to the child. The Mother and Father have loved one another since the beginning and the child is the result of Their love. So be patient; this new life is worth all of the suffering in the world. This new life is a life of love that words cannot describe."

Collin looked into her illuminating eyes and asked, "Are you an angel? Have you been sent here from God?"

The woman brought her hand to Collin's cheek and said, "We have all been sent here from God. We are all rays of the One Ray of Truth."

Then she turned to look about the park and continued, "All of these forms are from the same source… only sculpted a little different. The trees, the squirrels, the children playing, the parents, you and me… all from the same source…"

Then she looked back at Collin Hartley and said, "Soon you will see clearly the One in the many. You will see it without having it as an exercise of faith. The love that grows in you for the One does not compare to the love the One has for you. Through His mercy, His grace and His love, He will make you Realize you are simultaneously the Drop and The Ocean. The love you have for Him will bring you into His Oneness."

Collin replied, "In a way I fear that my heart is dying along with my body. I want to open my heart more but it feels numb. I'm scared."

"Be true to yourself," she said. "Look inside and find what truly loves. I know that if you search yourself, you will find that yours is not really dying. It's just that you're beginning to love in a new way. You are starting to realize the source of all worldly love. Your heart is not dying. It is changing."

"Yes," Collin said, "I'm finding love in the impersonal conscious experience. And through this, I'm finding that I even love the love of my animal heart. It also loves the contemplation of what it is. It loves observing within… it loves what is without… but it is quieter… more subtle…"

Then to Collin's surprise the woman suddenly sprang to her feet and said, "Enough talk! Let's dance!"

He just watched her at first while she began swirling like a dervish. The woman seemed like a gyroscope of perfect balance and symmetry as she spun round and round. Then she spun away from Collin and made a path for herself through the park. So Collin stood up and followed her though he did not join in the swirling himself. Instead, he followed her lead as she cut across the park and towards the corner of Leland and Clark.

The woman stopped the spinning near a stop sign where she began a new series of movements. Collin remembered the movie, *Meetings With Remarkable Men*, where the viewer is shown examples of sacred temple dances. And as she crossed the street she expressed, what seemed to Collin, some of those same sacred movements that he'd seen in the movie. Then she stopped in front of a door and waited for Collin to come stand beside her.

When Collin caught up, he noticed that they were standing in front of a bar room door. He heard the Johnny Cash song, 'The Man Comes Around', playing in the jukebox inside. He also listened as the patrons sang along and whistled into empty beer bottles. And before the song ended, the two entered into this urban honky-tonk.

The atmosphere of the bar brought back many memories into the presence of Collin Hartley. He remembered the drinking binges, his bar crawls and his promiscuity. He also remembered his hangovers, his black eyes and his adulteries. Collin had never been married. He considered his inability to stay faithful a sure sign that intimate relationships were a failure. He did not know how to love exclusively. He did not make the steps through monogamous relationships that would help his heart mature and grow. Marriage was not part of the plan for Collin Hartley.

He had been with many women in his life, but there were only two that were lasting relationships. He had lived with each one of them and neither of these partnerships worked out. Again, Collin found it impossible to commit. He felt incapable, in his youth, to maintain a lasting relationship with a woman. Collin was mostly in love with the abstract view of freedom. He wanted total freedom. His late nights at the bars and falling in love repeatedly was more appealing than developing a mature relationship with a mate. In his mind this was closer to freedom.

Meher Baba said, "Sinners are my debts. Saints are my assets. And I am eternally turning my debts into assets."

Collin and his angel took a seat on the floor near the bathrooms and Collin continued absorbing the impressions of the place. He inhaled the stale smoke and the spirit of Buffalo Trace. He heard glass beer bottles clanking as the bartender tossed them into the trash. He listened to the different conversations and stared into the yellowed eyes of the people encircling the central bar itself. Collin lived vicariously through their empty sips of Budweiser, Jim Beam and Jose Cuervo. He could feel the false courage and yet the inner fear that comes with an inebriated state. He could also see the beer muscles, as he used to call them, from two guys who were arguing about who was going to win the Superbowl.

Then Collin's angel asked, "Does this place make you feel uncomfortable, my love?"

He responded, "I feel a familiarity here… I feel like I know this place very well… like an old friend…"

Then she held his hand and said, "This is not you any more, my love. These are ghosts just like everything else in your past is a ghost. Life is changing constantly… one moment dark and the next light… one moment fresh and the next decayed… once dying and then living…"

"Yes," said Collin, "our life is so transitory. One minute we are this and the next minute we are that. We are forms flowing into other forms and leaving the images of ghosts in the wake. And I believe that you're right when you say that my past is a ghost. That's why I try to plough ahead without looking back. But then, here I am now… remembering things that I haven't thought about in years."

"Please don't judge this place, my love," the woman replied. "Remember that these are all just shadows. And not just the ones you see here. The children playing in the park and the people here in this bar are all shadows."

"And what about us?" asked the man Collin.

His angel did not reply to him through words; rather she communicated something unspoken through her being alone.

Then a server approached the pair and asked them what they'd like to drink.

"I'll take a tequila," said the woman.

Collin looked at her a little startled and then thought for a few seconds whether he should order a drink himself. He knew that he wouldn't get a 'real' drink but still, it had been five years since Collin had tasted a drop of alcohol, so he was hesitant about ordering.

"He'll take a Buffalo Trace on ice," his angel said, "and I would also like some salt and lemon with the tequila. Please…"

Then Collin's angel thanked the server and looked back at him as if to say that everything would be just fine.

Collin said, "I was in this same bar once several years ago. It was just after I moved to the city. I came here with some friends and we rambled on for hours about God, the creation, the fourth dimension and the 'real' purpose of life. I thought of myself as an agnostic back then… I was cold, cynical and too much in my head… I would sometimes even blaspheme against God and all the religions of the world. Blaspheme against the people who loved me as well. Drink after drink and cigarette after cigarette… listening to myself as I discoursed vainly, pompously and with pride while I exalted myself above others. Ego in full bloom."

Then Collin paused for a moment; he turned his head downwards out of shame and continued, "And I feel now that I am a living testimony of one important point expressed in the New Testament."

His angel remarked, "For whoever exalts himself will be humbled, and whoever humbles himself will be exalted."

"The Lord's discipline," replied Collin, "and even for someone who never believed."

It was then that the server returned with their nothings and laid the empty glasses on the floor between them. Collin paid the server while staring at both the empty saltshaker and the clean napkin that should have been a bed for the sleeping lemon.

"You are beginning to understand that there is only One Truth, my love. There are no believers and there are no non-believers. There are no priests and there are no atheists. There is no good and there is no bad. There is only the One."

Collin smiled as he felt hope in his conscious experience. Even the pains of his body seemed to slip away in the light of this hope. He sat with his angel in silence for a few moments all the while his mind was stilled and his 'beingness' was present. His consciousness moved between the dark catacombs of his inner self and then back out into the bar.

"It's still dark now," said the angel, "but the daylight is coming."

Then the two lifted their glasses and Collin Hartley consumed the emptiness of his past.

Chapter Seven: The Walls

Collin Hartley woke up. The sun shone down on him while he lay covered in his cocoon-like sheets. His eyes were closed but the daylight worked through his eyelids as if they were completely transparent. Before he opened them, Collin sensed his 'beingness' while lying there on the bedroom floor. He felt the slow pulse of his heartbeat and the tranquil rising and falling of his chest.

Collin Hartley's mouth was dry, his flesh withered but his blood felt fresh and clean. It seemed Collin's whole self was nearly immaculate. In fact, the morning itself was fresh in a new way. There were no odors, no residues and there was not even a hint of smells in the air. Neither good nor bad, Collin could only describe his experience as clean. Even his thoughts were clean as it seemed; that is, except for one tiny thought about Sunday morning pancakes.

Collin used to refer to his Sunday mornings as the Meditation of Pancakes. He would make wheat pancakes as a meditation and prayer for the sun. It was also a practice for getting beyond the influences of the sun. Collin was inspired and in love with the great Indian Sadguru Upasani Maharaj. In an old discourse, he suggests this very same Meditation of Pancakes.

Upasani Maharaj told his lovers that on Sundays they should meditate on the sun itself and that anyone aspiring to get beyond the sun, to merge with God, should practice the Meditation of Pancakes. He taught them that all the laws governing life on earth are directed by the sun, so he gave instructions to his lovers on how to get free from these laws. It was an exercise in total freedom. He told them that the secret to getting beyond the sun was to first understand the mystery of how the sun was created. He suggested the Meditation on Pancakes because, in the process of making the pancakes, the creation of the sun was revealed as well as an individual's means for liberation. He also instructed them to be simple, humble and heartfelt in this exercise.

So this meditation works in three phases: the first is the mixing of the wheat flour and water, the second is the creation of the pancake itself on a skillet, over fire, and the third is the consumption of the pancake. The aspirant was directed to meditate deeply through all three phases while also praising the sun for the life, light, warmth and beauty that it gives. The aspirant was told that they would reap the benefits of this practice over time but only if they remained humble before the sun and only if they were qualified enough, consciously, to receive a new understanding.

So Collin's thoughts remained turned towards the sun as it illumined him in his bedroom. Of course, he also thought about the pancakes and how nice it would be if he could have them for breakfast. And that was just it; it was the idea of the meditation of pancakes that was most appealing. Collin felt that it was not necessarily the real action of eating the pancakes that he was missing, but it was the idea, or thought, that seemed more appealing. And as the sun continued to shine on him, he imagined himself dissolving into it and then going beyond; he saw himself shaped into a perfect circle and then his inner man consumed it.

When Collin finally opened his eyes, he was astonished to discover that the sun shone freely into his bedroom since all of the walls and the ceiling had totally disappeared. He sat up while the branches of a tree swept across the far corner of the bedroom and scraped against the floor. Collin smiled as the wonder and fascination of this new information flooded into his presence like a mighty wind.

He looked about the apartment and saw that the only structural aspects that remained were the floors, the doors and the staircase. Then he jumped to his feet to see if the back porch was still there. His sight shone through what used to be a closet and even further beyond what used to be the walls of the south room of his apartment where he could see clearly that the back porch was in fact still there. Then a few birds flew past Collin and he turned his attention back to the bedroom. Tarazina made a leap for these birds and she almost went off the edge of the bedroom floor.

Collin rushed over to pick her up and exclaimed, "Whoa, girl! Be careful! The walls are gone…"

He held Tarazina gently in his arms and continued, "Ahhh, the walls are coming down, girl. There's no more separation… no more blocks put up… no more personal space…"

He sighed and looked deeply into her eyes, "Soon you will be gone. You and Willie are my last two great loves and connections to this dream."

As Collin petted Tarazina, he looked about the neighborhood without restriction. Just like his own home, all the homes within his eyesight were without walls or ceilings. He noticed some people racing around barefoot in the streets like he did the days before. He saw families pretending to have breakfast in their homes and he saw others pretending to sleep in comfortable beds. The only structural elements left in all the buildings were the floors, doors and staircases. The sky was clear and the daylight bathed the whole neighborhood in radiance. There was endless visibility and endless possibilities in sight.

Then Collin walked out into the living room and put Tarazina down on the floor; he petted her head and it was then that he noticed the neighbor from across the hall. Collin had never seen this woman before. He never bumped into her in the stairwell and he never saw her coming or going from her apartment. In fact, Collin even wondered if there was anyone living across from him at all. And he felt a little awkward since she was only wearing panties and a thin satin nightshirt. Collin could see himself as a peeping tom then, but he couldn't pull his attention away from her beauty and presence. Her long brown hair fell like silken sheets over her shoulders and the curves of her body accentuated the brilliance of each movement. It was obvious that she couldn't see Collin as she took the last empty sip of her coffee and walked back towards the kitchen. Collin Hartley followed her as he walked towards his own kitchen, all the while his heart was pounding with passion and awe for this woman. And his desire for her only intensified as she put her coffee cup into the sink and then walked into the bathroom to undress. She pulled the tiny garments off of her body and it was then that Collin's lust set him ablaze.

He could almost feel her soft skin, her full breasts and her moist lips pressing up against him. He kept staring as she brushed her hair in front of what used to be a bathroom mirror. Her hips were cocked to the right and the movements of her arms were like falling water as they waved and rippled with each stroke. Brush after brush and stroke after stroke, the woman combed through her hair. All the while Collin looked at this woman as the snake of sexual desire transformed itself into a dragon. His blood coursed through his veins like streams of fire and his mouth began salivating like he was a hungry dog. Collin's heart almost burst out of his chest. However, just when Collin's animal-self reached a maximum, his inner man subdued the dragon and he turned away from her in embarrassment. The shame and pangs of conscience washed completely over him.

It was then that Collin's guilt appeared. He walked into the east room of his apartment with his head tilted downward as he felt the sting of guilt by intruding into his neighbor's private life. But after a few moments his shame stole from this guilt and then the carnal passions dissolved altogether. Collin's inner man was recovered and his animal-self was domesticated through the whole process. The dragon soon transformed into a snake, then the snake transformed into an egg, and the egg finally transformed into a speck at the seat of his physical body.

Interestingly enough, what remained in Collin Hartley was the pure beauty, awe and liveliness that he experienced from seeing this woman. All tendencies to have her as an object of desire were completely resolved. But within him, in his interior man, the beauty moved throughout his self as an unspeakable energy that he had never known. At that point he was beauty, he was awe, and he was alive with indescribable currents of energy that reverberated outwards toward the surface of his flesh. The appetite for sex and possession were totally vacant.

Collin Hartley took a seat on the floor and continued looking downward was he contemplated how he would manage the remainder of the day. He could see by this most recent experience that it was going to be challenging to carry on with any normalcy since he was now able to see into the personal lives of those around him. He even felt some fear as he could imagine some of the darker sides of human nature that typically stayed hidden behind the very walls that had now disappeared. He questioned how he'd respond to the terror that some people are capable of since things were now becoming unveiled. He thought of the sexual abuse, the domestic violence and the outright pure animal deviancy that happens in some homes. So Collin questioned whether it was better to keep his eyes on the ground throughout the day or if it was more important for him to see whatever came to him naturally. To all of this he had no definite solution, only a new perception and a new life that he had to live regardless of his decisions.

After his considerations, Collin crossed his legs, closed his eyes and prepared to spelunker through the dark catacombs of his inner experience. However, to Collin's surprise his inner space was much lighter than he expected. As he attended to his breathing, he noticed a vastness and depth to his inner life that he'd never witnessed before. In one way it seemed that he had developed new eyes within himself and they peered about in this open-inner space. These new eyes were different than his old eyes; these new eyes did not have to move about in order to perceive in one direction or another. These new eyes did not work to focus on special forms or objects; instead, they attended to the quality of inner light alone. So these new eyes worked to perceive light where his old eyes worked to perceive objects. And in the same way his old eyes brought him closer to the various objects of desire, Collin's new eyes brought him closer to his inner light. Collin Hartley went through the stages of his morning exercise, the whole time giving special attention to this inner light. This experience was interesting as he could still feel himself in the cave of his inner life yet there was also a sense of movement and the flaring of a faint and indescribable light.

When the morning exercise was finished, Collin Hartley drew open the shades that were his eyelids and began perceiving with both sets of eyes simultaneously. The outer eyes attended to objects like the computer, the cat and the doorway where the inner eyes attended to the quality of light alone. Collin worked to stay focused on his apartment without catching glimpses of the events occurring outside. So he moved his outer eyes about while his inner eyes stayed present, and through this he felt a union of his inner and outer man coming together. At that moment Collin Hartley felt two pieces of the only puzzle that existed coming together and forming one. His conscious experience grew through this union and the result was a new state of being.

Collin dressed himself in the bedroom while he felt moments of wholehearted love for The Unseen. Collin could have sworn that the Divine even breezed through his heart at times. This made him feel clean from the inside and it was as if his inner chambers were fumigated by The Divine Presence. He continued to put on his clothes as the cool air moved about freely in the bedroom. The spirit of the spring was still there and with it the freshness of all things coming back to life. So Collin Hartley didn't need the oil that Willie had given him that morning.

Before Collin left the apartment, he saw the neighbor again from across the hall. He couldn't help but notice her as he walked towards the front door of his apartment. She was fully dressed now, aside from the bare feet, and she sat on the floor of her living room doing what appeared to be homework. He turned his eyes to the ground as he passed through the doorway. Collin kept to himself until he reached street level.

When Collin exited his building, he heard the sounds of clapping feet everywhere. It was just like the day before where all of these sounds created a symphony of sorts. There was layer upon layer to all this stomping, flapping and shuffling. Then as Collin walked, he added his own part to the ensemble. This chorus was a perpetual motion of rhythm, tone and melody, and Collin Hartley was tuned into it with every step on his path.

Collin decided to take a long walk to Renee's rather than sprinting down the train tracks as he did before. He was excited to meet Willie, but he knew that he had plenty of time before the visit. Collin always appreciated his Sunday meetings with the Mysterious William Green, since they made up for the breaks they took on Saturdays. It was agreed upon, a few years earlier, that Saturdays would be a day apart for them, so Sundays were of special value. The work week was absorbed and digested by Saturday, so Sunday was a time for sharing results. These were the days when Collin shared the consensus of his falls and successes with Willie. Sundays were also generally longer meetings between the two where they not only enjoyed one another's presence but also the coffee and atmosphere of Renee's itself.

As Collin walked through the north side Chicago neighborhoods, he tried to keep his sight downwards and his attention directed at himself. He didn't want to invade the private life of those around him, so he made efforts to contain consciousness within himself. This was difficult as he still had to function in a world populated with diverse peoples and events. Collin had to take care not to bump into other people while walking and he had to remain perceptive enough not to get trampled when he crossed the street. However, when Collin walked through the dark shadows of the northside he couldn't help but observe what was going on there.

Collin Hartley heard cracking, screaming and grunting coming from one of the buildings he walked past. When he looked at where these sounds came from, he immediately regretted looking at all. Collin saw a woman chained to the floor of a garden apartment; she was scarcely dressed in leather while two men struck her with wooden canes. The three were smiling yet all of them screaming at the same time. Their pleasure and pain both combined in a twisted display of sexual amusement and all this disturbed Collin. So he quickly crossed the street as his empty stomach became queasy. He almost ran from what he'd seen but then another gruesome sight awaited him on the other side.

Collin saw a father yelling at his daughter in a kitchen. She stood in front of an empty plate with a flat affect over her face. This little girl couldn't have been more than eight years old, and the father verbally abused her as if she were his worst enemy.

He screamed, "I told you to eat it, you ungrateful little bitch! You don't choose what you eat around here, Princess! Now, I want you to pick up that damn fork… you stick 'em in those damn potatoes and you eat 'em!"

The little girl shook her head expressionlessly, then Collin watched as her father beat her. The man wouldn't let up as he pounded her furiously with his fists, even when his wife jumped on his back in an effort to stop. Collin stood there as the tears filled his eyes and as the sense of cowardice came over him. He was paralyzed on the spot and he couldn't move. It was like an invisible force held him in place and would not allow him to turn away. It was only after the father walked away that Collin had free range of motion again. So he stumbled away from that scene and reminded himself not to be consumed in judgment.

Collin Hartley stopped and leaned up against an oak tree. He looked up to the sky and said, "This is your creation, Lord, and I will not judge the Acts of it. This is your Divine Play and I know that your righteous judgment reigns supreme. The limitation of my mind cannot explain what seems to be injustice, cruelty, and inequality."

And Collin meant every word that he said. As much as these events disturbed him, he knew that it was not his place to judge them. Collin believed in the omnipotence of God, he believed in His all seeingness and His all righteous judgment in everything. Collin also believed in the laws of karma and that every person creates debts and credits to their account in life. He also understood that these karmic accounts get settled in this life and new actions create karma for the next life. The transmigration of the soul includes karma moving from one life into the next life. If a soul is coming out of the animal form and into the human form it brings the animal karma into the human life. This includes animal passion, animal possessiveness, animal cruelty, and animal love. So these thoughts gave him perspective and clarity in his perceptions.

As Collin headed further south, he had the good fortune of receiving an opposite set of impressions. The majority of the people in the neighborhood that he was now in showed nothing but love and a strong sense of community. He smelled the spirit of backyard barbecues, he heard families laughing together and he saw friends helping each other with yard work. Collin saw disputes being settled and he saw lovers making up on the steps of their front porches. And Collin Hartley couldn't help but believe that this was the overall consensus of the world. It seemed to him that this must be the way the majority of people on the planet Earth live their lives. He felt that if it were any other way the earth would simply die and wither away. However, the earth was not dying; she was only changing a little and it seemed to Collin Hartley that she was perhaps getting ready for a new experience in her love life.

A few blocks before reaching Renee's, Collin passed a currency exchange where he saw a familiar face. It was Adam, the man he talked with on the train earlier in the week. Adam was looking up at the sky as if completely drawn into its endlessness.

Collin approached him and asked, "What words could describe the freedom of the blue sky?"

Without looking at Collin he replied, "To even try explaining it is an impossible limitation. Even these same words coming out of my mouth right now are an impossible limitation. These words that acknowledge the inadequacy of descriptions are nothing... they are empty... impotent and limp just like words that we use to describe the sky..."

Collin stood next to Adam where they were both now peering up into the blue beyond together. The spirit of spring only added to the intensity of this moment and their period of silent appreciation was a quiet offering to the creator.

After a minute or so Adam asked, "How are you, Collin? How is the experience of your life?"

"I'm taking everything that falls to my lot," said Collin. "I'm working with my experience as best I can. I'm trying to stay present and I'm trying to be completely human through all of this. Trying to be a man in the full sense of the word."

Adam turned to Collin and asked, "What does it mean to be a man in the full sense of the word?"

Collin explained, "I believe that a real man takes whatever falls to his lot without argument, without complaint and without asking why. He openly accepts the whole variety of experience, which of course includes the good, the bad and the ugly. To be a real man means that he bears his suffering quietly and he welcomes any and all chances to be humbled. I believe that a real man loves his Father and does not question the ways in which he is disciplined or rewarded."

Adam smiled and responded, "This sounds more like the description of a saint than that of a man."

"Perhaps," said Collin, "maybe that's what a 'real man' is. Maybe the 'real man' is a saint. Maybe he's even more."

Adam looked back to the sky and said, "We really are blessed with these various trials and countless opportunities to develop the qualities of man that you're talking about. Without these tests and trials, we would not be able to experience the Highest. We would have no way of getting qualified for the Divine Life."

Collin responded, "It seems impossible to get free from earthly bindings and head in the direction of the Divine. I see that my animal-self doesn't want to give up its connection to the objects of desire. It doesn't want to lose the good food, the beautiful women, the walks in the park... My animal-self still seeks these things even when it's starved of them. So it sleeps at times... but it needs to be killed altogether..."

"Death comes slowly to the beast," said Adam. "It doesn't happen instantaneously. The animal in us is powerful and its constitution is remarkable. However, our inner man is much stronger, and this is the 'real man' that you were describing. The 'real man' can slay the beast, the dragon and the entire legion of thieves if he so desires. But only by the grace of The King and only after the inner man has become a 'real prince'. Man can do nothing alone. God drives the entire waking process."

"And to say that all of this takes courage is an understatement," replied Collin. "I'm mostly a coward. I'm fearful and I have doubts. I really don't want the things I love taken away. Actually, I have my faith out of necessity. To cope with things being taken away outright. Or just having my relationship with the things I love changing."

It was then that Adam turned to Collin Hartley and slapped him across the face. Collin was totally stunned as he brought his hand up to comfort his right cheek. He tasted the blood as it moved freely amongst his teeth and gums. In that moment Collin was also struck with great clarity and he openly turned his other cheek to Adam. So Adam gave Collin a crushing blow with a closed fist and Collin Hartley staggered as his balance was completely thwarted. The only reason he didn't fall to the ground was owing to the grace of a passer-by who caught Collin in his arms.

This older man looked at Collin, surprisingly, and asked, "My goodness, son, are you all right?"

Collin held the man's arms tightly and then nodded his head that he was fine; while the man held Collin, he looked at Adam in the eyes and said, "I don't know what gave you cause to hit this man, but I'm calling the police regardless!"

Then Collin suddenly pulled away from the man and told him that the police would not be needed. He thanked the man for preventing his fall and then Collin stood to face Adam again.

"You're stronger than you think, my brother," said Adam. "No man that's cowardly or fearful can accept a blow like that one. It's only your doubt that stands in the way now."

Collin remained silent while he looked at the ground and tasted the blood in his mouth. He could see the shadows from the group of people that surrounded the two, but he paid the gestures of concern no mind.

"I told you that we'd meet again," Adam remarked. "Those who are on The Way converge together. This is a law. So I won't say goodbye to you now either. Only, I'll see you again soon."

When Adam walked away from the scene, a few people approached Collin Hartley and tried consoling him. They asked if he wanted them to call the police or take him to the hospital to have his jaw looked at (he of course declined all these offers). Then Collin heard the older man who broke his fall explaining the whole story to new arrivals. And when the attention to this scene reached a climax, Collin Hartley walked away in the direction of Renee's.

As he got within fifty feet of the restaurant, he could see the Mysterious William Green sitting next to his bicycle towards the back of the wall-less space. Willie was in his lotus position and his bike remained totally intact. When Collin reached the front of the restaurant, he considered walking straight through the invisible wall. He thought it might be an interesting experiment. However, Collin decided against this impulse and he passed through the front doorway like everyone else.

As Collin neared Willie within the space of the restaurant itself, he was amazed by the illumination. The Mysterious William Green seemed on fire with white gold emanations surrounding his body. When Willie reached for his coffee cup, it joined this illumination as it too became part of the white gold aura. Then Collin noticed that Willie's eyes seemed dead: they were coal black and they appeared to be almost withered away.

Collin looked at Willie's forehead to see if there was any physical indication of a third eye, but there was none. When Collin went to sit across from the Mysterious William Green, he could feel the resonance of a new state of being. He felt very subtle vibrations, almost electric and cool in nature, move throughout his own flesh. These vibrations radiated from Willie and Collin Hartley partook freely of this communion.

Collin said, "It seems that there's almost no restriction to my seeing. That is, there's no restriction to what I see out here. The walls have now fallen so I can see everything. But my inner seeing is a whole different matter."

The Mysterious William Green was motionless and his black eyes hung on his face like onyx. Willie resembled an ancient sculpture that was hidden deep within a timeless forest. He was the type of artifact that would provoke different responses from different people. Some would see him as a horrific figure made by devils. Those same people would say that he was cursed and that he would curse you for being in his mere presence. Yet others would see him as a holy relic and they would observe him closely in an effort to discover his mysteries. Collin Hartley saw him like the latter and he experienced the familiarity of the friend as well.

"When I close my eyelids," said Collin, "my new eyes seek out the light. But inside me is mostly dark so these new eyes strain to see even the suggestion of light."

Then the server came over to pour the two some fresh nothings and she didn't seem aware of Willie's transformation. Collin thanked her for the service and then she pitter-pattered away with naked feet.

Collin continued, "And when my eyelids open, I perceive the world with two sets of eyes. The outer ones attend to material objects and the inner ones look to light alone. This is new for me and I feel like I've been adjusting to it all morning."

Collin paused for a moment to sip his emptiness and then remarked, "I've also been adjusting to the disappearance of the walls."

And it was then that the Mysterious William Green responded to Collin Hartley, only he used hand gestures instead of words. He raised his hands with the backs of them directed at Collin. The pinky fingers of each hand were touching each other as the hands themselves made a wall. Then Willie broke them apart vigorously as his arms made a single wavelike motion. It reminded Collin of a movement that a musical conductor might use while directing an orchestra. Then Willie laid his palms flat to the floor and nodded his head.

Collin was quiet at first while he pondered the symbolism of Willie's hand signals. He felt, most of all, that Willie expressed the breaking apart of one thing and the subsequent free reining of something else. He thought maybe this was about something that was once contained now being released.

Collin said, "I feel a climax being reached myself, like a balloon that's been filled to the limits of its capable expansion. And the only way for release is if the balloon bursts or if some of the air is let out of it."

Then Collin looked to the Mysterious William Green for a reply but there was nothing. So he continued, "I can't know The Truth with my mind yet I still try. And my self-doubt somehow stems from this oddity. The action of my mind trying to understand what's beyond it causes the feeling of self-doubt since another part of myself knows that this is impossible. And I feel this self-doubt strangling me at times."

It was then that the white gold aura surrounding Willie moved closer to Collin Hartley. It didn't quite touch him but it did move nearer to him.

Collin closed his eyelids and said, "I want to move towards The Unseen and at times I feel a real step in that direction. This is a very distinct type of movement and I know this step is real. The problem is that I take one step towards The Unseen and then one step back towards the world of objects. And I also know that there are many steps that need to be traversed but I can't seem to make it beyond the first. Again, I shuffle back and forth… one step towards True Light and then one step back to darkness…"

Collin kept his eyelids shut and it was then that the Mysterious William Green spoke to him. And to Collin Hartley's astonishment, it was inside himself where Willie shared his words. It was like having a conversation inside of a cave where the voices were soft yet they still echoed.

Willie said, "The one who finds himself alone in the wilderness has two choices and the one he picks depends on his courage or lack thereof. The courageous one seeks 'a way' to 'the path' that will bring him home, and the one without courage stays paralyzed in the very place he found himself. So the courageous one has hope whereas the coward has none. If the courageous one is wise, he will survey the lay of the land and search for 'a way' to 'the path'. If God is on his side, then he may even get directions from the spirits or he might find the footprints of others journeying on 'a way' and he'll follow their trail. And if he succeeds in trekking his way out of the jungle, he will find himself on 'the path' that will take him home. However, none of this will be easy. Remember that he is alone in a dark wilderness surrounded by wild animals and in constant danger of pitfalls. This wilderness is also densely overgrown and there is very little light to guide him along the way. So this courageous one also needs to be patient, he needs to stay attentive constantly and he needs infinite endurance while he proceeds. There are no guarantees for even the bravest who find themselves in this position but without these efforts they will rot away in this same jungle."

"So you see the position that I'm in," said Collin. "You are here with me now in the darkness. I know that I must find a way out but I'm struggling to do this by myself."

Willie replied, "The only way to make it out of here alive is for you to use your own two feet. No one can take these steps for you. You must walk yourself. And indeed… you have walked a long way…"

The two turned silent so that only the sound of breathing could be heard in the inner cave of Collin Hartley. It was a rhythmic echoing of inhalations and exhalations. Then Collin spoke.

"In a way I feel close to 'the path' but in another way I feel far away."

"Just keep ploughing ahead," Willie responded. "Don't look back and don't stay put for too long. Remember that you're either ascending or descending. You're either going towards God or away from God. In the end everything disappears into the Light."

Then a flare of fear came over Collin and this shook the inner walls of his cave. Small pieces of stone fell from the ceiling and the floor of the cave grumbled like an upset stomach.

"Be gone!" shouted Willie. "To the grave with you! Go back into the abyss from which you came!"

As the Mysterious William Green spoke, the fear vanished from Collin Hartley and the cave became still. Collin could even see a soft pulse of light coming from further inside himself. His new eyes attended to this light as he spoke to Willie.

"The fear still comes and goes. Especially when I feel something powerful is present. I have a habit of interpreting this power as something evil and bad."

Willie replied, "And this will prevent you from advancing further on 'the path'. You must stop interpreting power in its destructive sense. At this point. Don't even think about 'the path'. You've been on the path. You are almost home."

Collin, who remained fixed on the inner light, said, "I'm still working to discern between what's real and what's unreal. I'm trying to step towards truth and walk away from lies. But as I told you before, it seems like I take one step forward and then one step back. It's like I make a move towards the mysterious and then a step back to the all too familiar."

"I told you to stop looking back," said Willie. "You only think this shuffling of your feet is happening because you're absorbed in a memory of the past. Be here now, Collin, and see The Spirit that moves in All Things. Daydreaming about yesterday will only paralyze you in the place you're standing. Clouds the seeing."

Then Collin Hartley opened his eyelids and saw that the Mysterious William Green remained seated across from him like a statue with the white gold aura still surrounding him. Collin watched as Willie brought his hands together like a pyramid with the tips of his fingers showing the apex. He held this position for a moment and then he ascended the pyramid to just below his own eye level. Then Willie broke them apart with the same wavelike motion he used in the earlier hand gesture.

Collin absorbed the wonder of the Mysterious William Green's presence while still sensing the electrical vibrations, from the aura, moving about his self. Collin felt real life and at this point, the withering away of his flesh meant nothing. This new life was consuming the old one, so his flesh was reduced to being a meal. This experience went beyond the food chain of the material world where The Truth of what was inside Collin Hartley fed off of the physical man. And the vibrations he sensed were the 'coming to life' of The Truth. This Truth did not have the same restrictions and weight as the life he had once known. This Truth was radiant, formless and light.

Then Collin Hartley stood up and tossed his money on the floor next to his coffee cup. He said goodbye to the Mysterious William Green and then left out the front of Renee's.

Collin stood on the sidewalk there and observed the entirety of his surroundings. The people were still barefoot and running around the streets as if driving cars and riding buses. The melody of these feet clapping still sounded all around and now it mixed with the birds chirping, people talking and children playing. Then Collin looked into all of the wall-less buildings on Belmont Avenue. He saw people sitting on the floors eating their nothing and enjoying the love of one another's company. He looked to The Bed Zone where the salesman, Al, talked to potential buyers of phantom beds. Then Collin Hartley looked down at his own bare feet and noticed some blood dripping on the tops of them. It was then he remembered being struck by Adam, so he brought his hand to his lips to wipe away the blood that fell from them.

Suddenly, Collin was struck by a new vision of the world and in this vision, he saw the life of the planet completely transformed. He saw men and women reducing their animal selves to lean donkeys that subsisted on small portions of hay and water. He saw the consumerism, the cheap laughs from television sitcoms and, in fact, the American dream all withering away to nothing.

Collin Hartley saw the divine man and divine woman reigning supreme in this new life of the spirit. He saw the food chain become non-existent; the fish, the cattle, the lamb and the sow roamed free. And the spirit of The Divine formed a new humanity of true brotherhood and sisterhood like something the earth has never seen before. Collin heard new music, he saw new art and read the words of new literature. This new life was one of spiritual adventure, a life of mysteries and a life of real community. He saw new temples being created by the manifestation of a universal mind. And people did not build these temples with their hands and raw materials; instead, these temples were created through divine vision alone. So the callousing of hands and the straining of muscles became something of the past. In a way this vision even became indescribable as Collin experienced images that he could not express in words and indeed in this new life, all the languages of the world disappeared; the language of The Spirit reigned supreme.

So Collin Hartley walked home in a state of elation while he whistled along to the Johnny Cash song, 'The Man Comes Around'. He heard the voice of the man in black in his inner ears and he felt his love for God in the center of his being.

Chapter Eight: The People

Collin Hartley woke up. And he would have opened his eyelids that morning if they were not transparent. Yes, Collin Hartley's eyelids were see-through so there was no need for him to open them. He saw the daylight, the birds flying overhead and the shadow of a tree next to his bedroom branching out over his face. Collin saw a few clouds advancing slowly above him and he saw the tip of his nose pointing up towards the blue sky. Then he brought his hand before his face and saw that it was transparent as well. Collin saw just the faintest hints of flesh and bone, and the rest of his hand was luminous like the white gold light that surrounded the Mysterious William Green. Then Collin sat up and looked at the rest of his body. He could see his enlightened upper half disappear into the sheets that covered his lower self. So he pulled the sheets away and then experienced his enlightened whole.

Collin came to his feet and moved to the edge of his bedroom to look out at the neighborhood; it was then that he realized that all the people had vanished. The streets were empty and silent, and all the wall-less buildings were void of human beings. The only forms of animal life that Collin could see were birds, squirrels, dogs and cats. But there were no families, no children, no wives and husbands and no pitter-patter of feet. There was only the profound quiet emptiness of a world nearly dissolved, and if it weren't for the few faint sounds of the birds chirping and Tarazina purring, the world would have seemed dead altogether.

Collin's cat purred while she rubbed herself against his illuminated ankles. She looked up at him and begged to be picked up. So Collin reached down and lifted her up to his side.

He said, "This is it, ole girl... the final disappearing... everyone has defected to a new land."

Then Collin kissed the top of Tarazina's head saying, "So I guess it's time that I join them."

Collin Hartley put her down on the floor and then took off his boxers and running shorts. He knew that there was no need for these things now, so he pulled them off and tossed them into the clothes hamper.

Collin looked down at his naked luminous self in wonder and it was then that he understood he was becoming immaculate. He didn't need to wash himself off since he was nearly spotless from the inside out. He could still see the hints of flesh and bone, but they were now bathed with inner light. It seemed he had undergone a cleansing by fire and now that he was clean, it was time to discover his formal wear so he could enter the wedding feast. The clothes of the flesh were ready to drop. The True Luminous Self was ready to blossom.

It was then that he heard the dinner bell. It sounded in the air, in the ground and into the man Collin himself. The ringing resonated into everything that remained like the crystalline chiming of wine glasses. These chiming vibrations were powerful yet subtle, and they played into Collin like a beautiful violin whose music makes the soul weep in ecstasy. This created new emotions in Collin so that he felt beauty, love and a bliss that is impossible to communicate through words.

Collin could see that everything left in the creation was on the verge of vanishing. He envisioned the apocalypse where the sky and earth were ripped wide open to expose the truth. So there was a kind of brief terror in this feeling of tearing away all he'd ever known, but there was also a feeling of anticipation and longing for the exquisiteness that was behind it all.

It was at that moment Collin first cried out, "Is that you, God!"

And this wasn't so much a real question as it was a real seeking out of the unseen. These were the words of the one crying out in the desert, and he wanted directions to be led home.

Collin Hartley descended the stairs in his building and walked out naked into the barren streets. When his feet touched the concrete, he could feel the pulse of the earth's heartbeat. It thumped and echoed like a drum while he walked towards the train tracks. The city of Chicago was a ghost town, only there was no wind-blown sands and no tumbleweeds. It was a phantom in its own unique way. The tenants had only just departed so the feeling of their lives still remained. He could almost hear some of their voices and he felt the faintest sensation of warmth left on the sidewalk by their bare feet. When Collin looked down, he noticed that his body did not cast a shadow. He was self-illumined so he saw his own light project down onto the street as he walked. Collin was free in all of this; he was free in light and free in his walking down the street. There were no obstructions, everything was opened up and the creation was getting exposed for what it really was.

When Collin reached the train station, he ascended the stairs and took in the view of the city from the platform. The great crystalline vibrations still penetrated everything that was left and Collin could even smell this. It was the cleanest and most refreshing scent he'd ever experienced. It was an indescribable cool smell; it had no specific aroma and yet it was uplifting beyond words. As this chiming continued, the planks of the train platform began to shake. In fact, the whole earth was reverberating with it. This earthquake was terrifying yet astonishing at the same time. As Collin looked out over several city blocks, he was even sure that everything remaining would collapse and be consumed by the earth. However, everything stayed as it was while it pulsed with the continuous vibrations.

Then Collin called out again, "Is that you, God!"

There was no response; only the complete knowing that he was on the verge of vanishing into the unexplainable. The last vestige of his individualized ego and separate existence was about to disintegrate. This kept the emotions of fear and wonder on the forefront. They were like two trembling stones holding up the temple of Collin Hartley. Take them away and Collin would crumble to the ground. The fact of this temple falling was indisputable; it was now only a matter of moments.

It was at that point when Collin jumped onto the train tracks and started walking southbound towards Belmont Avenue. He walked at leisure through the middle of North Lakeview. The man Collin was splitting the world in two and he observed what was on his left and right while he walked. To his left was all of the good that remained in the world. It was to the left that the sun was hanging, the birds were flying and the wind was blowing. To his left the trees were home to an abundance of life and it was to his left that all things pleasurable were found.

Then Collin looked to his right which was the world in shadows. The clouds loomed to his right and some even fell upon the trees as a fog that suffocated them. To his right the world had become completely lost in a haze of gray mist and it stunk of mildew. To his right was the sadness and it was to his right where pain was found. Then Collin looked directly forward and the vibrations of the unseen penetrated through both sides. The left and right, the pleasure and pain and the life and death all got struck by the crystalline chiming. All of this apparent variation was consumed by the mystical ringing.

As Collin walked on, the reverberations continued to intensify. The foundations of the creation were shaking loose and he felt that the train tracks could collapse at any moment. And though Collin was terrified he knew now that Into His Father's Hands was the only place that he could fall. He was realizing that there was no other place to fall. There was only the One and he was merging into That Formless One.

So when Collin reached Belmont there was practically nothing left of his limited self. The only remaining particle was his desire to see the Mysterious William Green one last time. And even this was only a minor desire since he could feel The One in Willie and The One in himself. This was the last threshold of the final annihilation of Collin Hartley. He descended the stairs and then walked out onto a desolate Belmont Avenue. He stood in the middle of the street and observed the void around him. He looked to the far east and the far west and there was nobody. Only the chiming and the wind sounding like a singing voice at times.

Then Collin Hartley looked straight up into the blue beyond. He was ready to vanish and swim his life away in those clear blue waters. Collin was nearly as pure as the sky itself; there was only a paper-thin film separating the two and even that was about to disappear.

"Is that you, God?" he shouted upwards into eternity.

Again, there was no response; only the incredible sense of The Unseen Presence. In that moment there was no big and small, no infinite and finite and no understood or misunderstood. There was only 'presence' and 'being'. The indescribable essence of life and love itself was there and there was no quantifying or understanding the Truth.

Then Collin Hartley looked into Renee's Restaurant. He became somewhat grounded again, yet he was still free in spirit. He saw Willie's bicycle propped up on its kickstand and just beyond it was a single door with white gold light shooting out from all around it. Collin walked in through what used to be the front wall of Renee's and moved toward the door. As he passed the bike, he gave it one last glance. It remained exactly the same way Willie had altered it. Collin touched the handlebars and then turned his face towards the door. It was majestic and the white gold light from behind it bled out and joined Collin's own inner light. He drew his hand away from the bicycle and then took a few more steps so that he was right in front of the door. Then the light from behind the door and the light from within Collin Hartley mixed with the universal chiming as it all reached its climax. There was an apocalyptic exhale of relief and The Ocean of Love embraced the light of Collin Hartley.

"Is that you, God?" Collin asked quietly once more.

Who am I?

I am

Who am I?

I am

Then the ground shook, the door quivered and Collin Hartley turned the doorknob. He opened the door and then disappeared completely into the Infinite Effulgence of Light.